BATTLE MAGIC

BATTLE MAGIC

THE LEIRA CHRONICLES™ BOOK 12

MARTHA CARR

MICHAEL ANDERLE

LMBPN Publishing
PMB 196, 2540 South Maryland Pkwy
Las Vegas, NV 89109

First US Edition November 2020
Version 1.02, January 2021
eBook ISBN: 978-1-64971-301-8
Print ISBN: 978-1-64971-302-5

From Martha

*To everyone who still believes in magic and all the possibilities
that holds.*

To all the readers who make this entire ride so much fun.

*To Louie, Jackie, and so many wonderful friends who remind me
all the time of what really matters and how wonderful life can be
in any given moment.*

*And finally, a special thank you to John Nelson of the Austin,
Texas Police Department who patiently answers all of my
questions. I hope I made you proud. Thank you for your service.*

From Michael

*To Family, Friends and
Those Who Love
To Read.
May We All Enjoy Grace
To Live The Life We Are
Called.*

CHAPTER ONE

Leira laid down flat on her belly and leaned under the bed. "Almost..." The running shoe was just out of her reach. "Son of a..." She pressed her lips together and let a little energy flow through her. "Fuck the house rules." The shoe came spinning toward her, landing neatly in her hand. "Got you."

She sat up just as her phone rang, rolling over and brushing off dust clinging to her arm. Blocked number. A smile spread across her face. "Hello General Anderson. It's been a minute since I've heard from you. I've been wondering how you're doing without Patsy and Lois."

There was a soft chuckle and a groan. "Well... Sometimes you realize the value of an asset after they're gone. I'm afraid this is one of those times. But I'm heartened by knowing Lois is leading the Silver Griffins."

"With her wing woman."

"Yes, I sent over a bouquet of candy to congratulate them" said the general, with a laugh. "They are an indomitable force. I'm calling with an unusual assignment."

Leira smiled again, pressing the phone closer to her ear. The general was never one for chitchat.

"There's a scientist, Dr. Alan Petrie, giving a TED talk on immunotherapy and curing cancers today in Chicago at the Wirtz Center on the Northwestern University campus."

"Fascinating. Why does he need a bounty hunter? Is he a problem?"

"He doesn't need one, but there's someone hunting him who will be a big problem."

Leira leaned back against the dresser. "Clearly I'm missing part of the story since you're not relying on the local cops."

"It's a little complicated but I'll break it down for you. Dr. Petrie's work could not only teach the body to cure itself of cancers but of any mutations that don't belong."

"Damn, that only took a full minute to cross into Wolfstan Humphrey territory."

The general let out an annoyed *tsk*. "That vermin. Maybe you'll be relieved to know he's not the problem this time. This story doesn't have the tangled roots of Mr. Humphrey's machinations. Dr. Petrie used to have a partner working on the project with him. Dr. Lane Jeffries. She was a noted biologist. Unfortunately, there was an explosion during an early experiment that took out the entire lab and set back their research for years. Dr. Jeffries was presumed dead in the aftermath of the fire."

"No remains to prove it?"

"It was a blue fire and only a few pieces of burned metal survived. It was thought that there was an artifact involved but to this day Dr. Petrie has sworn that he has no knowledge. That was all ten years ago before we met. Here's the twist."

Leira sat forward, her arms resting on her raised knees.

"Dr. Jeffries is very much alive," said General Anderson. "But not exactly the same anymore. The doctor now has the ability to drain people of their memories when she makes contact with them. It will even cross through clothing. The government has her classified as a new kind of magical but I'm not sure I agree."

Correk walked into the room with the troll on his shoulder. They were both chewing on the ends of a red Twizzler stick. Leira narrowed her eyes glancing up at them.

"A kind of truce," whispered Correk. "I'm sharing... some."

Leira pulled the phone away from her ear. "It's General Anderson with an assignment."

Correk nodded and turned to go, but not before Yumfuck had filled his cheeks with the Twizzler making them bulge out to the sides like a chipmunk. He smiled at Leira, his pointy teeth encased in licorice. Leira smiled and waved, the troll still bouncing on Correk's shoulder and waving back.

"Leira? Did you hear what I said?" The general cleared his throat, clearly annoyed.

"I heard every word. How did you find out Dr. Jeffries was alive?"

"Dr. Jeffries showed up at the lab at University of Chicago in Hyde Park shouting about revenge. An added twist, she doesn't look to have aged a day. She left a guard and a professor with everything intact but their personal memories. A strange and selective mutation."

"Bad time for Dr. Petrie to be giving a TED talk, unless you're trying to draw out Dr. Jeffries."

"Let's hope Dr. Jeffries doesn't see through us as easily as you just did. She's dangerous..."

"And could expose magic, I get it. Has anyone figured out who threw the wrench into the experiment yet?"

"That is still unresolved and another piece of the problem. For now, we need you in Chicago today. I'm sending a file on both doctors along with the coordinates. You'll be met by two of my people who have been instructed to only observe."

"Got it," said Leira, standing up and brushing off the last of the dust. "I will capture someone I cannot touch."

"She's had no close contact that we know of with any real magicals so we don't know if the effects would be the same but use caution. You have too many good memories to let them go easily."

The general was gone before Leira could reply.

Leira sat on the edge of the bed and put on the running shoe. She went downstairs and found Correk sitting at the kitchen table. Yumfuck was sitting in the center of the table licking a pat of butter. "Now what?" Leira screwed up her face watching the troll. The troll looked up at her, his face shiny as he smiled.

"He won a bet, and this is what he wanted," said Correk with a shrug. "I really didn't think he could eat that many Twizzlers at once."

"Sucker's bet," smirked Leira. "Aim higher, troll. Maybe a taco or a burger next time."

Yumfuck cackled and gingerly licked the butter. "Yum... butter."

Leira shuddered and shook her shoulders. "Suddenly an assignment on a rainy day seems like a good idea."

"Where to this time?" asked Correk, trying to look away as the troll pressed the pat against his face and sighed.

"Chicago, but with a stop first. You know that room in Turner's house that creates clothes based on need and desire? I need an outfit that could contain an artifact if it had to."

"You're chasing after an artifact? We have bags for that."

"I'm chasing a human who's become an artifact." Leira ran her hands down her sides. "I need something that won't let her energy pass through, just in case."

Correk studied her face for a moment but said nothing.

"I'll be back before you know it," she said, putting her hand under his chin and kissing him on the lips. She leaned her forehead against his. "I've been tasked with retrieving a lost soul that needs help, with a little bit of dangerous magic mixed in. We've faced worse."

"I get it. Be careful and come home soon."

"Of course. We're going to stop Wolfstan Humphrey and sooner rather than later. I know that's what's on your mind." Leira went into the hallway and opened a portal that lead to the main hall of Turner Underwood's house.

"It won't be easy," said Correk, taking a long look at Leira.

"But we'll find a way, or we'll damn well make one."

On the other side of the portal the old Fixer poked his head out of his library and came strolling out when he saw who it was. "Leira! How delightful."

Leira stepped through and waved to Correk as the portal closed behind her, sparks skittering across an ancient Persian rug.

"I need a favor..."

CHAPTER TWO

Leira sat in the balcony of the theater to the right, looking down at the small circular stage. She was wearing non-descript black slacks and a white shirt with a wide collar. Worked into the weave was a thread enhanced with magic. Turner Underwood had overseen the production, loudly stating a spell and waving his cane. Leira had done her best not to roll her eyes at the theatrical production and in the end had stifled a laugh with her hand.

Two agents were posted in the wings on either side. Everyone else had been cleared out and the doors backstage locked from the inside. Behind Leira was the lobby and the only entrance still open.

Dr. Petries stood in a spotlight on the stage, fluidly gesturing with his arms as if he was leading an orchestra. "In less than five years it will be possible to track through DNA what mutations a person may encounter. Then we can program their cells to defeat it long before the enemy shows itself."

He paced slowly back and forth across the stage, the

audience following every move. Leira scanned the area, keeping her magic on a low level, just enough to trace the other magicals in the room. There was a cluster of Light Elves sitting in the middle just below her, and two Witches off to the right side. *This time, that may not be enough to find you first. Are you even a magical, Lane Jeffries?*

There was rustling in the rows behind her and to the left. An older man got up and was making his way out of the aisle as everyone pulled in their feet. Leira could feel the hum of magic coursing along the back of her neck. Something wasn't right, but the more she scanned, the more normal everything looked.

"That's the problem," she whispered. "Dr. Jeffries knows how to blend with the crowd." *I need to look at everyone differently.*

Leira looked again, her lips buzzing from the energy poking at her from the inside. It could sense something. *There.*

A young woman in a puffy coat lingered at the entrance. A hat was pulled down tight on her head and her hands were stuffed in the pockets. She started to come down the aisle just as a handful of students laughing and jostling each other headed toward her.

She got out of the way, pressing herself against the wall until one of the students glanced over at her. "You alright?" he asked, but she looked away. Her mouth opened slightly, a purple electrical current dancing across her teeth. *Got you.*

Leira got up and followed her out as the woman headed to the lobby and turned toward the orchestra section, taking her time. She was carefully maneuvering to keep her distance from everyone. Leira closed the gap between them still keeping a few feet behind her. The hum along the back of Leira's neck grew, making her concentrate to hide the energy and not let her eyes glow.

As they came into the aisle on the lower level there was sudden applause and Dr. Petries paused, waiting for it to die down as he smiled, looking out over the audience. The woman in front of Leira stopped and curled her hands into fists at her sides.

She got closer to the stage and looked down both sides, like she was searching for a seat. Dr. Petries noticed her and became distracted, losing his place for a moment. He squinted into the audience, but the spotlight was making it difficult for him to clearly see anyone.

"Lane Jeffries." Leira said the name loud enough for Dr. Petries to hear. The young woman startled and turned around to glimpse at Leira.

Alan's eyes grew wide and sweat formed as he stepped back, making his forehead shiny in the light. He looked to the left and right for assistance.

Dr. Jeffries peeled off her hat and took the stage in one easy movement, even as Alan Petries' backpedaled, his hands out in front of him. He was stuttering, "No... no, no, no." The words echoing over the audience from the speakers. Several of them were starting to rise out of their seats. Leira ran the last few yards and vaulted onto the stage, shaking her head with a stern look at the agent who stepped out of the shadows. His hand was grazing his gun. Ushers came from the sides and began pushing everyone to quickly leave, emptying out the theater.

"Don't do this," said Leira, in a stern but calm voice. "I

don't believe you want to harm anyone. You were doing your best to stay away from those students."

The last audience members made their way out the door and the ushers took their positions, blocking the exits. Leira could finally let the magic flow up her spine and out through her arms.

Lane whipped around, her face contorted in anger. "They didn't cause this!" She held up her hands as the same purple current jumped from finger to finger. She stretched out her arm, pointing at Petrie. "He did."

Alan shook his head wildly. "I swear I didn't."

"Liar! You were so worried about the funding if the experiment failed." Lane curled her fingers and held her hands close to her chest. Her eyes were shining. "You didn't even have the decency to be there when I started the experiment."

Leira carefully watched Alan Petries open and close his mouth. A fish caught out of water. "What makes you think Alan Petries could have done this?" asked Leira. "Where would he have gotten an artifact like that?"

Lane took another step toward him, the electrical current making the skin on the back of her hand ripple. "That's how I know it was him," she snarled. "Before he was a full professor, he was an assistant one summer, but in the anthropology department. He needed the money."

Alan slowly closed his mouth, swallowing hard, his eyes still wide.

"He came back from a trip to Egypt bragging about the dig and hinting that he had managed to keep something for himself. No one believed him, but I wondered." The electrical currents around Lane's body picked up, circling wider and wider around her chest and waist. "I went by your office before I came here. I had to know for sure and I knew all eyes would be over here on you. The bowl was gone."

Alan blinked hard several times, still glancing to the left and right, but the agents didn't move. Leira took another step closer, sliding the gloves out of her pocket that Turner had also made for her. She slipped them on, stepping around Lane till she was almost standing between Lane and the source of her anger.

"He deserves this more than anyone. He lives off memories that are part lies, part truth." Lane spit out the words. "Imagine if all he's left with are the lies." She lunged for Alan, swinging her arm as he stepped back and tripped, falling to the ground. Leira stepped in front of him just as Lane's fingers grazed her shirt. The electricity crackled brushing up against the spell. The smell of something burning hung in the air.

Alan moved his arms and legs frantically behind Leira as if he were trying to swim across the floor. "I had no idea that would happen. It was meant to be a boost, even a favor to you! You would have succeeded, we all would have won. Why would I purposely try to hurt you?"

Lane's hands were shaking. "What are you?" she asked Leira. "You're not normal either."

"Very subjective term, I find. I'm mostly a Jasper Elf." Leira's eyes glowed. The small patch of skin visible on her wrists showed symbols flashing over and over again.

"What? Magic is real?" Lane looked confused, shaking her head. "How is that possible?" She fell to her knees as a relieved Alan Petries, crawled toward the side of the stage and out of reach. He was stopped by an agent who placed a heavy hand on his arm, shaking his head at him.

"I was kind of where you are now and not that long ago. But there's also a chance where you are can be reversed, if you let me help you." Leira waited patiently, remembering what it was like the first time magic had entered her life.

Lane seemed to regain her strength and rocked back on her heels, pushing herself to a standing position. "No! What about him," she said, pointing at Alan. "He has to pay!"

Leira moved quickly to stop her as Lane shoved her hard in the chest and ran past her. The shirt crackled again, snapping loud enough to make everyone wince. Leira felt the air rush from her lungs and memories spin in her head. Queen Saria in the castle, her mother's wedding, Correk injured on the battlefield, Mara coming out of the world in between.

But the fibers held, melting together and the memories stayed intact. Leira took a chance and slid forward on her knees, grabbing at Lane's ankle with one of the gloves. She pulled Lane off her feet before she reached the agent or Alan who was cowering behind him.

Leira heard a tap-tap right next to her and glanced up at a familiar face. Turner Underwood tipped his bowler to her even as he opened a portal. "You hold on to her a moment longer and we'll take her back to my place where it's safer for everyone, including Dr. Jeffries."

Leira scrambled to her feet and quickly grabbed Lane's arms from behind, pulling her backward till she was upright enough to shove toward the portal. The gloves sparked and tingled the entire time till she let go, dropping

Lane to the other side. The doctor rolled across the shiny wooden floor of Turner's study, coming to rest by the desk. Leira stepped through and leaned back to yell to the agent. "You'll hold him on charges?" The agent nodded as Leira ducked back inside, letting the portal close.

"I had it under control," said Leira, an eyebrow arched.

"That never has anything to do with accepting help," said Turner, keeping the end of his cane firmly pressed against Lane's back. "Stay down there. Don't make me use this," he said, sternly. Lane looked up but gave in and rested her head against her arms. Her cheeks were wet with tears. "Can you really help me?" she muttered.

"One way or the other," said Turner. "You'll either leave here and return to your old life. Or you'll learn to harness this new ability and investigate what else you may be able to do. Either way, it'll be an adventure."

Leira crouched down close to Lane, making sure to keep a little space between them. "Alan will pay for what he did but through the courts or the Feds." She nodded to Turner to remove his cane.

"My life has been destroyed," said Lane, rolling over and propping herself up on her elbows.

"Your old life, maybe. And if it is, you'll learn to build a new one."

"Where am I, anyway?" She sat up and looked around at the bookcases that lined the walls, bulging with books.

"In a magical world, inside a magical world with the best possible magical person to help you navigate whatever comes next."

"I'm flattered," said Turner Underwood, searching the bookcase for a particular book. "Ah, here it is. This will give us a place to start." He waggled his eyebrows. "Leira, you can leave us to it."

"What do you want me to tell General Anderson?"

"That the magical world has decided to take good care of one of its own." He looked at Lane. "If that's what you are now. Better we try to solve her situation than let the Federal government try to learn more at her expense." He tapped his cane, creating a portal for Leira to her hallway in the townhouse. "Go on, we have work to do. You will be called if needed."

Leira gave a crooked smile and stepped through the portal. "How do you keep getting through our wards?"

"I look forward to you figuring that out some day," he said with a smile as the portal closed, sparks dashing across the wood floor.

CHAPTER THREE

Louie retrieved the sword from the old umbrella stand and gently pulled it out of the sheath. "You sure you're up for this, Ronnie?"

The Gnome carefully took off his bowler and brushed off the top, setting it on the linoleum counter. "Don't get ahead of yourself. I've been fighting off Wizards since before you were born. Mountain Gnomes are trickier than Kilomeas."

"Okay, Ronnie. Keep telling yourself that." Louie lifted the sword ready to practice.

But Ronnie was on him in an instant. A blur of color zipping across the living room and giving a short chop to the back of Louie's knees. Louie crashed hard, banging against the wood floor. "Fuck you, you little..." Louie was sure he heard the sword give a short laugh.

Ronnie zipped back, standing near the door. He waggled a finger at Louie. "Now, now. Not nice to call me little. I can be back over there to punch you in the neck if you keep it up."

Louie rested the tip of the sword on the floor, pushing himself back upright. "What the hell was that?"

"I've been keeping that one in the chamber for a while, waiting for the right moment. You're getting soft. Girls'll do that to you."

Louie's eyes lit up and his face reddened. "You're off base," he snarled, swinging the heavy sword up to his shoulder. *Steady.* The sword spoke to him in a soothing tone.

Ronnie grinned, his stubby, wide hands on his hips. "Oh, now this is different. Could it be that someone of the female persuasion has actually managed to catch your attention for longer than an hour?"

Step forward. Louie took a step, gently swinging the sword in front of his body, pushing Ronnie back. *Lunge to the right.*

He moved his arm in time to cut off Ronnie's path, surprising the Gnome. "Okay, not bad. But how much of that is the sword?" cackled Ronnie, slipping past him and biting him on the arm before ducking behind the kitchen counter.

Louie finally smiled, twirling around, his blonde curls damp with sweat. "Biting? That's what it's come to?"

Ronnie slowly poked his head out. "Imagine a Kilomea taking a bite like that. Suddenly it's a real weapon. You have to pay more attention, dude. It's hard to break in a best friend and I've put a lot of years into you." Ronnie let out a roar and shouted, "Durius et ferro!" His skin took on a metallic sheen and he barreled straight at Louie, bowling him over. The sword clattered to the ground.

Louie raised a knee catching Ronnie in the gut and rolled him over, pressing his arm against Ronnie's neck, trying to reach out for his sword. The lamp on the nearby table rolled toward the edge, distracting Louie as he grabbed for it. Ronnie saw his chance and bashed Louie in the side of his head with his armored limb, sending him to the floor.

Neither one noticed the sound of a key carefully turning in a lock and the door opening just a little. Ava stood in the hallway, peering in the sliver at the Wizard and the Gnome wrestling on the floor. Her mouth hung open and her eyes were wide as she took it all in, not saying a word.

Louie tried to get back to the sword, but Ronnie pushed it out of the way with his foot. That gave Louie just enough time to roll the other way and pull out his wand that had been conveniently taped to the underside of the couch. He whipped it around in a semicircle, propped up on one elbow. "Sounds of birds. Jangled nerves." Louie jumped to his feet in one swift motion.

Ronnie was busy pressing his hands against his ears, his eyes shut tight. "Low blow, son of a lizard! Are those woodpeckers?"

Louie circled behind Ronnie, keeping an eye on him. "Woodpeckers and angry blue jays. Give up?"

"Never!" Ronnie gritted his teeth and opened his eyes just in time to catch sight of Louie. He used Gnomish magic to zip himself around the exterior of the room and attack Louie from behind. The racket was still loud between his ears as he jumped on Louie's back. "Make it stop or I bite off an ear!"

Ava pressed her face closer, mesmerized by what she was seeing.

Louie was spinning around trying to knock Ronnie off but to no avail. He flicked his wand, elbowing Ronnie at the same time. "Novis," he finally said, bringing the racket to an end. Ronnie slid off his back, sweating and breathing hard. "I could have taken you down just now."

"Really? You're gonna go there? We can start again if you want," said Louie, smiling. "Man, you really bit me!'

"Gnomes don't play. How about we call a fifteen minute truce and drink a beer?"

"I can do that." Louie waved his wand, opening the fridge as two long necks flew through the air and he easily caught both of them. He handed one to Ronnie and twisted off the top.

Ava pulled back from the door, holding her breath. She took a few steps back before turning in the hallway and heading back to the stairs without saying a word.

CHAPTER FOUR

Leira held up the pair of jeans and the stretchy dark blue yoga pants. "I'm not really a yoga pants kind of demon hunter." She dropped the yoga pants on the bed and slid into the jeans. "Remind me why I agreed to do this? I mean, I know Norah said we'd love it and it's good to hang out. No monsters, you know? I've never tried virtual reality, but we kind of live in one all the time. Correk?" There was no answer. She pulled a blue cable knit sweater over her head and went to the banister, yelling over the side. "Are you still here?"

One floor down she saw a flash of light erupt into the hallway coming from the direction of Yumfuck's room. His bedroom door abruptly shut, quickly followed by the tinny sound of hammering against metal. Correk's face appeared, leaning over the banister from the ground floor. "He's done it again," he growled. He held up fistfuls of empty snack bags, loudly crinkling as he squeezed them. "That rat bastard found my stash again."

"Didn't you see the flash of...? Never mind. Rat bastard seems a little harsh."

"I had Toblerone I was saving for a special occasion. And there were cookies a Witch gave me for helping her bones harden again." He waved the bags again, orange dust floating from one of them, catching the light as it drifted to the floor.

Leira grimaced. "Bones reharden. You do not have an easy job. Speaking of which, we have money now and can afford to always go and shop for more snacks, candy. Whatever your heart desires."

Correk came around and stood at the bottom of the stairs. "It's the principle of the thing. I even put a ward around the hiding place this time."

"Well, then you were just asking for it. You made it into a game with a troll. That's as enticing as a Dirty Old Bastard donut from Voodoo Donuts."

Correk arched an eyebrow at her but marched off.

"Hey, where were you hiding the stuff?" asked Leira, leaning out a little further. Correk came back into view. "I created a hidden door in the back of the pantry. I figured the smell from the other food would cover the trail."

Leira smiled at Correk. "It took him at least a few days this time. That's progress."

Correk wandered off again, muttering to himself. "I still can't believe one troll can eat that much. I know trolls. That's a lot of snacking. He should be exploding."

Leira went back and put on sneakers, grabbing her purse. She took the stairs two at a time, stopping on the second floor landing to listen. She heard a frustrated sigh coming from Yumfuck's room and she hesitated, her foot on the next step down. "You okay in there?"

"Yeah..."

"You sound a little defeated. You sure you're okay? Don't need an assist or another point of view?" Leira stepped close to his door.

"No... It'll be okay." Another sigh.

She pressed her hand against the door. "You having a rough day? Maybe I can help. Plans not up to code?"

The door opened a crack and she looked down at the tiny troll.

"Some days are harder than others," he said, squeezing his face into the crack.

"True that. I say this with some caution and only because you showed Mom and she didn't look worried. I'm sure whatever you're doing will work out. Maybe take a breather and go have some fun. There's no deadline, is there?"

"There is, sort of." He looked back over his shoulder and let out another sigh.

"Little fella, take a break and go find something else to do. If it still won't come together, ask for my help. Apparently, we can do that even when we don't need it. I got that from a reliable source."

Yumfuck looked up at her, his eyes wide and his paws clasped in front. Leira tilted her head and knelt down, scooping up the troll and hugging him against her neck. She could feel the soft fur stirring against her skin. "I'm here, Yumfuck. Never forget that. I love you. Correk loves you." She held him out to where she could see his little face and smiled gently at him. "When you're ready, I would love to see what you've been up to." She set him back down on the ground and a shudder passed through his body.

"When I'm ready," he said, sliding into his room and shutting the door.

"Bonding with a troll is harder than it looks," muttered Leira, "and worth it all day long." She reluctantly turned and headed down the stairs for the front door.

Leira stood with her new group of friends in the large powder blue rectangular room inside VR Zone. The corners and walls were well padded. Angel was standing next to her being unusually quiet, holding her headset and chewing her bottom lip. The teenage attendant wearing the maroon t-shirt with an image of a gorilla wearing a VR headset, was going over the instructions. Leira shifted the backpack on her back and took Angel's empty hand, squeezing it. Nicole bounced up and down on the balls of her feet. "Ready to go!"

"That's what we like to see! My name is Josh and I'll be your tour guide today to play in galaxies far, far away. You ladies are in for a fun day! Starship Enterprise is one of my fave picks. Who's gonna be the red shirt today? No takers? Just kidding. No need to worry," he said, giving Angel a gentle jostle. "Okay, the way this works. You'll be able to see the edges of the room. That'll look like the edges of the Enterprise bridge. Each of you will look like the avatar you have chosen. On the big picture window of the Enterprise the images will change. Does anybody else think it's weird that a spaceship had such a big window?"

He smiled and sighed trying to get a laugh out of the group.

Celeste was busy fidgeting with her goggles and Norah was looking around the room. Only Nicole and Leira were smiling patiently.

"Tough room," Josh muttered, still smiling. "Hey, sweet! You picked the battle action. Okay," he said, slapping his hands together and rubbing them. "There will be a nice battle sequence. I won't spoil the surprise. You will be given a chance to get your bearings and none of the ray guns really work."

Leira gave him a crooked smile and he gave her a wink in return.

"The game's gonna last thirty minutes and then you'll have another ten minutes to take selfies of your team to your heart's consent. Any questions?"

"Does anybody ever throw up from these things?" Angel pressed her lips together.

"Not so far, especially with the game you've chosen. If you feel yourself getting nauseous or lightheaded you can take a break. Anything else? Everybody ready? Okay, ladies, don your goggles and let's get this party started!"

Nicole and Celeste let out whoops as Norah and Angel carefully put on their goggles. Leira waited till everyone else was secure before she put hers on, adjusting the strap. Immediately, the surroundings changed to the bridge of the Enterprise. In front of her the large window showed a passing stream of rocks barely missing them. A planet in the distance glowed from the warmth of a nearby sun but was mostly red in color with a cloud of dust around it.

"Everyone find a seat." Leira turned her head to see

Josh's avatar dressed in a red Starfleet shirt. She let out a giggle and headed for the communications panel.

"Angel you take the command," said Nicole. "This was your idea, and you love yourself some control, girl."

"Go on, you can do it. I want to be the science officer. Nanoo, nanoo," said Celeste, holding up her hand with a V in the middle of her fingers.

"Wrong iconic show, Celeste," said Norah laughing. "I'll be the engineer. I don't know if we have enough dilithium crystals, Captain!"

Leira found her seat near the large window and sat down, reaching out toward the virtual screens popping up, feeding her information.

"Ready when you are, Captain," said Josh.

"Okay..." said Angel nervously, gripping the sides of the chair. "Warp speed ahead!"

Suddenly the image in the window changed and stars turned into blurred lines that felt as if they were streaking past them. Leira found herself pressing her head back against the chair. Magic swirled around her feet, curious and wanting to know more about what was happening. Leira took in a deep breath and pushed it out slowly, forcing the magic to settle down.

Bang! There was a loud sound followed by the sound of metal rubbing against metal. The large window tilted and Leira found herself compensating and leaning the other way.

The screen changed again as a large spaceship appeared in the distance. "That's a Vor'cha-class Klingon battleship! Deflector shields up."

"They are in place, Captain," shouted Celeste, letting out

another whoop. Her avatar turned and grinned at everyone. "Captain, you really know your Klingon."

Leira suddenly heard crackling in her headset and unintelligible sounds. "I hear something! Captain, we're getting a message but it's in Klingon."

"Command the dials in front of you to translate," said Josh in an excited voice.

Leira watched the virtual screen in front of her change as she said firmly, "Translation please."

The large screen blurred in front of them for a moment and then cleared to show the face of a Klingon Commander. "You have illegally entered our territory and hit our D-7 vessel. Someone must pay!"

There was a high pitched whir by the elevators as three images of Klingon warriors appeared to beam in from the enemy ship. Nicole pivoted, leaping out of her seat and firing at one of the guards just as he raised his ray gun. Leira swiveled her chair, watching the action and delighted that for once none of it was real. She could still feel the edges of her energy but was keeping it just out of reach enjoying the fun.

The Klingon avatars shouted at them in Klingon, interspersed with insults in English. Norah ducked behind her chair as another guard shot at her and she took a shot, missing him and burning a hole in the wall by the elevator doors. The guard fired again, grazing her shoulder and lighting up her avatar's shoulder. She sat down hard on the ground, still smiling but with a determined look on her face.

The warrior in the middle marched toward Angel who froze, her avatar's mouth hanging open. Leira stood up quickly and dove between them shooting off her ray gun and knocking the gun out of the Klingon's hands. Right behind that was her own magic, pouring into her arms and sending out a spray of small fireballs, lighting up the acrylic carpet inside the VR Zone room.

"Whoa! What the fuck just happened?" Josh was shouting and his avatar was running over to the carpet, stomping on the small sparks still remaining.

Leira could feel her face warming and she kept taking deep breaths as the Klingons froze right where they stood in mid-growl. Josh pulled off his goggles as his avatar froze in place too. "Did one of those guns actually fire?"

Leira pulled off her goggles and looked at the burn marks and Josh's sweaty face, his hair in tiny points on the top of his head. His eyes were wide, and he was walking around the damaged carpet. "That's impossible!" he squeaked. "They're not real."

Angel pulled off her goggles and glanced in Leira's direction. "Must have been something electrical," said Angel. "Cool special effect, though. I'd give this place five stars."

"At least," said Nicole, chiming in, still wearing her goggles and turning her head in every direction.

"We'll need to call this one early, ladies," said Josh, still shaking his head. "I can give you a partial refund and a coupon for your next visit. Man, that was actually making my heart race." He marched off toward the exit that lead to the lobby. The others slowly followed him, looking back at the mysterious burn marks.

Angel hung back near Leira. "Maybe next time we try

an underwater scene instead," she said, covering her mouth with a gloved hand.

Leira smiled, the lines deepening around her eyes. "Maybe my real life has enough alternate reality in it for now."

Angel nodded, chuckling and went to catch up with the others. "How about we get some wine to celebrate our victory over the Klingons! We actually managed to fire a shot that will be legendary in VR Zone lore!"

Leira took one last look at the damage and flexed her fingers. "That one almost got away from me," she muttered.

"Leira, you coming?" Norah appeared in the doorway, already out of her backpack. "Wine waits for no one." Leira trotted to the door, slipping out of her backpack as Norah put her arm around her. "Glad you're part of our brigade," she said, chuckling.

"Yeah, you've been baptized by fire," crowed Nicole. "No turning back now."

Angel smiled at her and gave Leira a thumbs up.

"Yeah, I'm part of the brigade. Let's go get that wine," she said, smiling. *A new home, at last. I've got to write Estelle.*

CHAPTER FIVE

Wolfstan Humphrey sat stewing in his office chair, overlooking a busy DC street below. "Damn them all," he muttered. He was gripping the pewter plate he had stolen, the edge resting against his lap. Next to him was a plastic bottle of water, half gone. The plate had shown him images of his future and the battle that was to come if nothing changed. But it kept refusing to show him the ending. He let out an exasperated sigh, glancing down at the scars left by the Willen attack, peeking out from his cuffs.

"What if I destroy Harkin's machine?"

He swiveled in his chair and set the plate carefully on his desk. He poured in an inch of water and blew across the top, a gold mist rising from it. "Yes, I could destroy Harkin's machine and end their quest." The Light Elf leaned over the plate and stared down at the water as images began to form.

There was a light knock at the door and the handle

turned, his assistant poking his head in through a slight opening. "Mr. Humphrey..."

Wolfstan's head jerked up and the images fell apart as the water formed a whirlpool in the center.

"Not now!" barked Wolfstan, causing the assistant to bang his head against the wall, trying to abruptly shut the door before removing himself. "Okay, well, okay..." he muttered, extricating himself and gently pulling the door tight. Footsteps could be heard after that, running down the hall in the opposite direction.

Wolfstan gritted his teeth, forcing himself to calm down even if it was only by the slightest of hairs. He blew a puff of air across the top of the water again as the shimmering gold reappeared. Images took shape once more and he leaned over the plate, watching anxiously.

Grey smoke billowed in the image, parting enough for him to see the building holding the machine lay in ruins. Fire was pouring out of the windows. "At last," whispered Wolfstan, his heart beating faster. But the smoke cleared further, and he saw strewn across the battlefield were his soldiers laying on the ground. Leira Berens suddenly appeared standing between the few remaining soldiers and Wolfstan's view, looking straight at him.

He took a closer look, his nose almost touching the water and noticed that the soldiers on the ground had black smoking circles on their backs. The ones still standing were running from him, not toward Correk, who stood in the distance. He was making his way through them to stand by Leira's side. At the last moment, Harkin pushed him out of the way, heading toward his old cellmate with a determined look and a fireball forming in his outstretched hand.

"Wait," growled Wolfstan. "I shot them? I did this? Why would I take them out unless they betrayed me? That's impossible!" he shouted, spitting into the water. Leira threw a fireball at him, making direct contact as a bright light flashed in his face making him blink.

Wolfstan sat up, banging his hands on his desk on either side of the plate. A ripple appeared in the water. He picked up the plate and poured the water into his already wet trash can.

"One hundred different strategies and they all end the same. Damn you, Leira Berens. I will find a way to remove you from this equation." He choked out the words, a bitter taste in his mouth and a fire burning in his chest.

He poured another inch of water onto the plate and set a new intention. "I kill Leira Berens." There was a hint of glee in his voice. He blew across the water as a gold shimmer rose and eagerly leaned over the plate to take a look.

Nothing appeared. The water was clear and still. "I kill Leira Berens," he growled, blowing again and leaning closer. The water began to move, swirling around the edges. "That's more like it."

Suddenly, it took shape, the water forming into long, delicate fingers that rose up, swimming across Wolfstan's face in rivulets and running down to his neck. There the water circled around his neck, faster and faster, tightening its grip. Too late, Wolfstan realized what it was doing, and he patted at the water, splashing it onto his crisp, white shirt and red tie.

But he still couldn't take in any air. He fell back into his chair, his head rocking back and his eyes bulging out. "Darkness help me," he squeaked out, a black ooze dotting his skin. The water rolled off the greasy ooze, loosening till Wolfstan could take in a breath, gasping. The pupils of his eyes disappeared for a moment, turning jet black before returning to normal.

He sat back, shaken, water splashed all over the top of his desk. The plate was dry.

"What pact have you made about Leira Berens, and with who?" His voice was a rasp. The plate began to rattle on his desk, vibrating faster and faster till it turned to sand, reshaping itself into a small pile. Wolfstan's cell phone rang and when he saw who it was, he answered, the bitterness inside of him growing as fast as the anger. "Ariana, what do you want?"

"Enjoying your gift from the gala? I just received a trigger on a very old spell embedded in that plate. I was beginning to wonder if you would ever ask the question."

"Fuck you, Ariana. You have your revenge," he growled into the phone.

"Oh, I haven't even begun. You stole some of my own kind for your monster making factory. It's given me the perfect excuse to try out some of our older weapons. Frankly, all I have to go on is lore so this should be fun. Watch your back, Wolfstan Humphrey. You're not the only one doing the hunting and my aim is true."

There was a click as Ariana abruptly hung up. Wolfstan rocked back his head and roared, his energy rattling the large window behind him.

CHAPTER SIX

Wolfstan pushed the sand to the floor with his arm, resting his laptop on top of what remained. He typed in the address at the top and whispered a spell, the keyboard glowing purple. The magical dark web opened up in front of him. His hands shook as he inserted the thumb drive. A mixture of delight and malevolence bubbled up in his throat. He went to a message board frequented by magicals angry about the constraints of hiding magic. Only the Silver Griffins and the threat of Trevilsom Prison held them back from bringing magic out into the open.

It's a new day, he wrote. *And it's time for those of us who can bend magic to our will, finally take our rightful place on this planet. Why wait until the gates open? Most of us will be gone. Let's start today.*

The comments started piling in almost immediately. Gnome183 imagining what he would do if it weren't for the Silver Griffins. AlElf38 lamenting that there was so much power kept under wraps. *Imagine what the world would look like if we were set free.* One after another they spoke up, some angry about teasing them with the impossible.

Wolfstan's face twisted into a satisfied sneer. "I will have my way, yet."

Imagine no more, he wrote. *For those of you brave enough to take the challenge... Here are all the hidden Silver Griffin agents. Happy Hunting everyone and welcome to the new era of magic on Earth. Come out into the open and play.*

He attached the file, a giggle escaping him and watched with glee as the file was downloaded. Slowly at first, accompanied by doubters looking for the trap.

Who the hell is this? asked Wizard20.

Careful, there's probably a spell attached, wrote Elfof-Tomorrow.

But it didn't take long for the tone to change.

Hey, I think this thing's legit. Holy shit, wrote Gnome183.

This is going to change everything, typed another.

The messages piled in and others were tagging friends to come and look.

It didn't take much longer for the downloads to pick up the pace till it was in the thousands and climbing. "The end of the Silver Griffins is at hand. This is just the beginning of everything." Wolfstan leaned back in his chair, his hands crossed over his belly, watching the numbers spin. "If I can't have it all, then no one can."

Leira was sitting at the kitchen table with her feet on the opposite chair. Correk was standing at the stove making dinner. "Maybe tonight will be quiet," he said.

Leira's phone buzzed and she wrinkled her nose. "I think you jinxed it," she said, picking up her phone and reading the text.

Nine-one-one. Use a portal and meet me at the Carousel Lounge. Cousin Petie is waving his usual rules. Portal into the exterior. I'll be at the bar. COME NOW. NOW!

"Correk, I think there's a problem..." She looked up at Correk who had already turned off the stove and was standing still with a faraway look. "I have to go. I'll explain later," he said, kissing Leira quickly on the top of her head and rushing to the hallway. "Take the troll with you," he shouted back to her. The spatula sat on the top of the stove, dripping grease.

"What's happening?" she asked, but he was already gone, the portal closing with sparks skittering down the hallway.

Her hands tingled with energy and the symbols along her arms were already flipping over furiously. She heard the bedroom door above her open and close and saw the troll sliding on the banister, neatly jumping to the floor when he got to the bottom. A ridge of fur along his back was standing on end and he was trembling. "Something's wrong," he said.

Leira swallowed hard and held out her hand. "Come on, we have to go." She scooped him into her pocket and opened a portal to the inside of Carousel Lounge. The lights were dimmed, and the place was empty except for Cousin Petie behind the bar and Doc sitting on a stool, nursing two fingers worth of bourbon. There was another glass next to him and he slid it over without look back to see who had arrived. Leira sat down next to him. "Cousin Petie adjusted the wards. No one else is getting in here in the next half hour. Then this will become a refuge." Doc was hunched over his glass. He picked it up and swallowed the remains.

"I'll pass. It's easier to channel the energy sober." Leira slid the glass back toward him and sat down. Cousin Petie gave a nod and put down the rag he had been using to wipe the bar top. "I'll be in the back getting ready for visitors." He slipped past a beaded curtain in matching colors to the carousel.

"Why the emergency call?" Leira sat on the edge of the barstool. The troll poked out his head and looked around but didn't try to leave the confines of the pocket. He smelled the air as if danger had an odor.

"Someone has released the names of every hidden Silver Griffin agent in this part of the world." Doc rubbed the stubble on his chin, grimacing. "They're all in danger. I couldn't believe it at first when I saw it. The list is being downloaded by the thousands as we speak. There are too many to protect unless we come up with a plan and fast but even then, it may be too late. Help the ones you know personally and then we'll work our way out from there."

"Correk..." whispered Leira. She stood up, her hands on her hips, her bangs falling across her forehead. "I'll start with the ones I know from Austin and I think there's a few retired ones down the street from me in Washington."

"Bring them here. It'll make a good way station while we figure out what to do next. Cousin Petie will make a space for them."

"This is going to be one crowded bar."

"This is only one stop on an underground map for magicals. There are hundreds of others everywhere and it's going to take all of them to sort this out. Now go! I've already sent funds to your account."

Leira shook her head. "No, this one is gratis." Leira got off the stool and took a few steps back, opening a portal to the kitchen in the Jackalope bar in Austin. Jack looked up with a startled expression and ran to the swinging door to block it. "There are humans out there in the bar. What's gone wrong now?" he said in a hushed voice.

"Already done," said Doc Leahy, ignoring Jack. "You'd better go. Don't worry, you'll have earned the money before this is over."

Leira stepped through and let the portal close as Doc turned to watch, his face drawn into a scowl. Sparks danced across the linoleum floor of the kitchen.

"Jack, you still have that phone tree for agents in the area?"

"Of course. I don't know if you've noticed, but I don't tend to throw out much of anything."

"Activate it and give them these coordinates. Tell them to portal now with their families as quickly as possible. No time for questions or explanations. Whatever code you use for nuclear, use it and fast."

Turner Underwood stood on the train platform far underground beneath Chicago directing the fleeing agents. Two shiny red train cars were lined up, end to end, quickly filling with Silver Griffin agents and their families. Correk came rushing down the stairs, weaving in and out of the Witches and Wizards carrying belongings and holding on to small children's hands. He stopped to help a Witch with her suitcase as she picked up her small Wizard. They got to the train and squeezed on just in time. Correk put down the suitcase and stood back as the doors closed.

The first train left with a *whoosh*, disappearing down the tracks in an instant. The second train was almost full as well as others waited anxiously on the platform.

Correk made his way to Turner who was offering his arm to an older Witch. "There are wards on all the entrances," said Correk. "Only agents will be able to get through the wall in every Starbucks everywhere. The underground railway is secure for now, but it may not last. Where are we sending everyone?"

Turner tapped his cane on the ground as the second car left and two more came speeding in to take their place. Witches and Wizards from other locations piled out, making their way through the magicals coming down the stairs. Everyone had an anxious look on their faces but were moving quietly, making almost no noise.

"We are playing a dangerous game of chess, moving people around to places where they won't be noticed and can blend in with the background. There's been an elaborate plan in place for just such an occasion for a long time. But with massive plans like this there's no way to practice."

Another car sped off and still the agents kept coming.

"Let's hope it works." Correk looked up toward the entrance. "How is it that no one is noticing their absence from their neighborhoods?"

"I'm afraid they will notice. This may be the turning point." Turner doffed his bowler to a trio of Witches, placing it back on his head with a tap on the top. "Magic is about to come out in the open. Wolfstan Humphrey will have his way yet." Turner suddenly stood up straighter, turning his head to the right. "You'd better go. The bad element among us is hitting the streets. The distress calls are starting to come in. I will not be far behind you. If you have any injured, bring them to my house. We'll set up a field hospital there and in old New York. Get your father. He's a fine physician as well, if you'll recall. He can help." Turner went to Correk and put a heavy hand on his shoulder. "This is going to be our most difficult hour, but we will not fail because we cannot. Now go."

Correk waved an arm and was gone in a moment. A five year old Witch oohed in surprise, pointing and trying to get her mother's attention. "Did you see that? That big Elf just disappeared." She clapped her hands in delight as her mother picked her up, the child still leaning over her shoulder.

Turner waved to the young child and tipped his hat as he tapped his cane, disappearing in the same manner. The child squealed with laughter as her mother pushed onto the train and the doors closed behind them. The train pulled out with another *whoosh*, steam pouring from the car as more cars showed up to replace them, emptying out with agents pushing toward the stairs.

CHAPTER SEVEN

Lois ushered the last of the Silver Griffin agents out of the Water Tower building and stood at the entrance. The black patent leather purse dangled from her wrist. "Patsy?" She yelled toward the stairs. "What in tarnation could you still be doing? We need to get going."

Patsy appeared at the top of the stairs carrying two large Jewel grocery store bags full of candy. "It seemed a shame to just abandon all of it. We can take most of it home."

Lois rolled her eyes, pushing her glasses back up her nose. "You have the strangest priorities. Did you grab the picture of Earl off my desk like I asked, or did that get ditched for a box of Reese's cups?"

"I got it. Of course I got it," said Patsy, making her way down the stairs. They stopped in the lobby and took a look around at the old building. "It's a shame we have to leave her empty like this. They'll surely come and tear this place apart."

"All they'll get is brick and mortar. Every dangerous artifact has been moved and fortunately no one knows about the real vault," she said, patting the purse. "We left behind trinkets. Just enough to entice them into the building. Once they're in there, we'll send in agents to trap them. Trevilsom's gonna need a new wing on it."

"Maybe something with a nice ocean view," said Patsy, getting a laugh out of Lois. Patsy puffed up her cheeks and blew out the breath. "How long till you think they'll swarm the building?"

"I'd give it an hour tops. There are some who are as dumb as bricks and they think they'll catch us off guard."

"Erickson would have been a big help right now." She saw Lois' pained face. "I knew you were thinking it. His mind took a left turn to Albuquerque and just kept driving. But when he was sane, he was a good agent. We don't have to throw out the memories. Does anyone know where he is? He's gone quiet on us."

"I think it's sinking in for him, the scale of what he's done to his friends and family. He was never really evil, just poisoned by revenge. Are you ready for this old friend?"

"I have our supplies," she said, hoisting one of the bags. "This should last us at least a couple of days if we show some restraint."

Lois stared at her for a moment. "Your blood must be eighty percent sugar."

"You have all your wands with you?" Patsy shimmied sideways out the door with the plastic bags.

"I do, including the three-D model from the Feds. That

one is smooth," said Lois following her out. She pulled out one of the wands and waved it in front of the face of the building. "That should keep them busy for a minute and it'll let us know when they arrive. Have all the Team Captains reported back?"

Patsy put the bags down and pulled a wand out of her pocket, waving it over them. "Light as a feather, hope for fair weather. There." She picked them back up again and started walking next to Lois. "I heard from all of them and they're ready. The moment that ward goes off like a doorbell, they'll gather like a storm cloud and rain on their little parade. Should be fun."

"Strange times," said Lois, as they turned and headed east toward the lake. "We've never lived in a time when humans had a clue about magic."

"They'll get used to it. They always do. The question is how rough the reentry is gonna be."

"Erickson didn't do us any favors," said Lois.

"Well, traitors never do. He'll get what's coming to him. Karma never loses your address and neither do we. Where are you going to hide the purse?"

"I've got just the place in mind and it can sit there for a thousand years if it has to, till it's safe again. Lacey Trader would even approve."

"Rest her magical soul."

The long grasses in the fields along the edge of the Texas sanctuary rippled toward the wards protecting the vast acreage. They were being pushed back against the magical wall meant to protect them.

Wolfstan Humphrey was slowly and deliberately peeling back the wards till he could slip through and step onto the secure grounds. He was tired of looking for moments to seize the upper hand. None of them had worked out anyway. Best to go back to basics.

March through the front door, head down, shoulders squared. Weapons ready. He was muttering spells, fireballs dancing in his hands like small, fiery stones.

Once he was inside the wards, he was able to advance quickly up the hill and press his way toward the lab. His long dark coat was unbuttoned, flowing behind him in the strong Texas wind. The scars left by the Willens stood out in pale white lines along his neck and hands.

He stopped for a moment and sniffed the air for effect, searching the ground for traces of Harkin's magic. "The yellow brick road right back to you... and that damnable ring. Come out, come out wherever you are because I know you're here somewhere."

The wind moved through the trees, rustling the tops and disturbing the birds roosting along the branches. They took to the skies squawking and chirping, flying over the lab toward the deeper reaches of the sanctuary. Harkin looked up from the computer and glanced at Lily. "Something has them riled up."

A herd of iridescent reindeer pushed through the trees; streaks of glowing light passed behind a dense tangle of tall oaks.

Wolfstan came to the edge of the trees, magic surging through him. There were hardly any traces of Harkin's magic slowing his progress. Protection spells within the sanctuary pushed at him, testing his limits of magical skills. But he shoved back with brute force, ripping holes through them.

The ground underneath his feet shook as the animals ran away from him as if a tidal wave was approaching. They could sense the coming destruction.

But halfway through the forest the animals stopped running in a straight line, forming a V shape around an obstacle facing the other direction.

The Gardener of the Dark Forest sat up on the back of the large lion with antlers the color of the frothy ocean during a storm. He was just in front of and to the side of the lab, biding his time. He had waited for this moment and he could be patient a little longer. The enemy had finally come to him and he was going to relish destroying him. He pressed his heels gently against the ribs of the lion and held onto the mane. The vines curling through his dark hair transformed into snakes, hissing as they pulled back his long locks. The Gardener held up a long, weighty broadsword, pointing it straight out in front. He was watching the trees and the way they were moving, signaling one to the next the progress of Wolfstan Humphrey.

"For every animal that has suffered at your hands, may you pay the price in flesh and bone," whispered the Gardener as the lion began to move forward, weaving in and out of the trees without effort.

Wolfstan pushed his way through tangles of vines, briars catching onto his coat. He caught a spark here and there of Harkin's trail, but most had been thoroughly hidden by the Gardener's efforts. Instead, the remnants sprinkled along the ground were leading Wolfstan astray toward a clearing due north of the lab. He finally broke through and was met by the loud roar of a lion and felt a confusion pass through his body trying to reconcile the sound with the sharp points of the antlers that were tearing at his chest. He looked up into the fierce eyes of the Gardener as the lion reared back. The Gardener raised the sword and brought it down in one swift motion, taking off Wolfstan's right hand at the wrist like it was warm butter. The hand dropped to the ground and was immediately covered by the tall undergrowth, pulling it down under the soil.

Wolfstan blinked in surprise, his mind running on instinct, forming an escape plan. His one remaining hand conjured a portal opening to his house hidden deep in Crozier, Virginia. The Gardener lifted the sword again and slashed it across Wolfstan's chest in three quick, even lines. Then he shoved his boot into Wolfstan's chest, pushing him into the portal and cracking two ribs in the process. Wolfstan fell back, his arm and chest bleeding onto the thick Persian rug, quickly staining the design a deep red.

The lion placed his paw into the opening and the Gardener leaned forward between the antlers. The snakes wove their way in and out of his hair, hissing at Wolfstan. "Your time on this Earth is coming to an end, Wolfstan Humphrey. Watch everything you've done become your reckoning. Live to see everything turn to bitter ashes. The moment that happens I will come looking for you to finish what was started here. There is no place you can hide. There is no shelter you will find to keep me out. I will be the last face you see, Wolfstan Humphrey and the time is drawing nigh." He gently nudged the lion again and the great beast pulled his paw back, letting the portal close. Wolfstan Humphrey stared back at them, his face ashen and his eyes wide with horror. Left wounded and still without the ring.

CHAPTER EIGHT

The Gardener slipped off the lion and watched as the animal padded off into the forest. The snakes in the Wood Elf's hair had settled back into vines weaving his hair into a braid.

The Wood Elf made his way toward the lab, the undercurrent of the sanctuary returning to normal as the animals and birds moved back over the ground. A snake slid across his foot, making its way toward a rotted tree, disappearing under it. The Gardener paused, patiently waiting till lifting his boot and crossing the yard to the screen door.

He came inside, Harkin and Lily looking up from the workstation. "What was causing the commotion?" asked Harkin, his brow furrowing.

"A momentary distraction that has been handled," said the Gardener with a scowl. Harkin knew better than to push him further. Besides, he had other things drawing his attention. He picked up a small tool and walked over to the large, hooded machinery, making an adjustment.

When he straightened back up, he felt the strain along his shoulders but ignored it. "We're ready to try the experiment again." He glanced from Lily's anxious face and her hands knitted together, to the Gardener with his arms crossed over his chest. "To get to a solution we're going to have to be willing to fail over and over again. There's no other way."

The Gardener nodded his head. "Then we keep going." He disappeared out the door leaving Harkin and Lily to wait in the quiet, no one saying anything.

Finally, Lily broke the silence. "I don't think you see what an amazing magical you are." Her voice was barely above a whisper and when Harkin looked up at her startled, she glanced down at the floor. She brought her gaze back up and looked him in the eye. "How many of us would have the perseverance and the courage to keep going after so many years? We wouldn't have a chance against what Wolfstan Humphrey has done if it weren't for you. All those souls... they'd be lost forever."

Harkin opened his mouth and closed it again, his eyes wide as he stared at Lily.

Lily bit her bottom lip and her hands danced through the air as she talked. "I know how this kind of work is measured in the smallest degrees. Many people can work their whole lives on a project and their success will be measured in inches. You've brought your friend back..."

Harkin interrupted her, shaking his head. "I caused it in the first place."

"Let's tell the truth here. All of it. You saved his life. It was messy and had terrible consequences, but without you we'd be talking about Peyton in the past tense. And when things took a horrible turn you did something about it." She blinked back tears. "I admire you, Harkin."

Harkin sat down heavily in a chair. "Lily, the admiration is mutual, I assure you. You went back into work and spied on Wolfstan just because it was the right thing to do."

Lily brushed a tear off her cheek and smiled. "Well then, I guess we make a pretty good team." She swallowed hard at the sound of an animal bleating as the sound gradually grew closer. "Whatever happens, we do it together and we don't give up till the whole damn thing works."

"Lily Sharpton, you are one hell of a Witch. I can't wait to see what you do next." Harkin rose and went to hold open the screen door.

"If there is a next time," whispered Lily, as the Gardener carefully led in a large black and white heifer. Most of the Holstein's abdomen was replaced with moving parts visible through an opaque covering. Lily winced at the sight, pressing her fingernails into her palms.

"She was rescued from one of the labs," said the Gardener. "I don't think she has a lot of time left." He gently stroked her back, letting his energy wrap around her body, easing the animal's pain. "Take her," he said, stepping back near the door. Harkin cautiously stepped near the cow as she bleated again, rolling her head to one side, looking up at Harkin. "Let's see what we can do to help you." He pulled in energy, letting it rise through his body till his eyes glowed. "Morbi ut papilio. Quasi folium componere. Fugit velut puer." The cow rose in the air and he carefully moved his arms, gently positioning her on the bed of the machine. "Here," said Lily, handing him the syringe filled with chloral hydrate. He injected the cow and waited as she slowly drifted off to sleep, a shudder passing through what remained of her body.

"Make sure her sacrifice means something." The Gardener left quickly without looking at either of them, letting the screen door slam shut behind him.

Harkin gestured to Lily to help him put the hood in place. Pixies gathered at the window, flitting back and forth. Harkin checked every dial, every measurement. He cleared his throat and started the device, a buzz suddenly filling the air. Lily pressed her fingertips tightly to her mouth.

He checked the settings one more time and before he could think about it any longer, turned the dial. The machinery gave off a low hum and the neon blue line of light zipped across the surface from one side to the other. It was quickly followed by another glowing stripe three inches away, and then another and another. Once the entire space was covered, the stripes started from the other direction rapidly creating the familiar luminous blue grid. The hum gave way to a sizzle and pop. The pixies pressed closer to the glass to get a better look at what came next. Sparkles of light bounced off the glass.

Lily stepped closer and took Harkin's hand squeezing it as she continued to stare at the cow. Harkin let go of her hand and pulled her in closer under his arm. "Maybe this time..." he muttered, watching the glow move back and forth across the Holstein.

"It's taking longer. That's a good sign. The body is still regenerating."

At last the machine decelerated and the blue lines reversed themselves, removing the pattern. The sizzle reduced to a hum and eventually to a stillness that filled the room. The heifer let out a rush of air and its legs shook as if it was trying to run in its sleep. "It's like it's remembering better times," said Lily.

"Let's get this hood off," said Harkin, trying to keep the excitement out of his voice. They carefully lifted the hood, setting it aside as Lily let out a gasp. "She's whole again. It worked. Can it be?"

The pixies flew back and forth, tapping at the window.

"Did it work?"

"Is the animal still alive?"

"Can you save the others?"

Harkin saw the Gardener's shadow pass in front of the door, but the Wood Elf didn't try to enter the lab.

He looked more closely at the heifer and saw a slight divot in her abdomen. "Something's not right." He gingerly pressed his fingers along her belly as his expression grew darker. "We've failed again. The organs were regenerated but not to the right size. She can't be sustained."

"What do we do now?" Lily lightly rested her hand on the cow's head as the Holstein let out a gentle moo.

"The right thing." He loaded another syringe and gently inserted the needle into the cow's neck, slowly pushing the plunger. The cow's breathing became labored until it stopped with a heavy sigh. He heard the Gardener bellow in anger as the pixies buzzed in a cloud before flying away.

Lily grasped Harkin by the arm. "Wait, if the organs weren't the right size, that's not a failure of the machine. That's our calculations. We missed something. Do you know what that means? We can do this. If we can get that part right, we can do this."

"No Lily, it wasn't just our calculations. The machine couldn't gain enough power. We need to figure out how to help their bodies sustain the effort or it'll never be enough."

"Then that's our next step. We'll get there, we will. And when we do, we'll end Wolfstan Humphrey's monstrous dreams once and for all."

CHAPTER NINE

The meeting took place in a high rise along the Grand Concourse in the South Bronx. A steady stream of Light Elves and Kilomeas, hidden by glamours, made their way up in the elevators to the apartment on the eighth floor. A Dwarf named Sal was waiting for them. He had thought up the idea to work in teams to hunt the exposed Silver Griffin agents. A Kilomea entered the apartment to find Sal standing on a hastily made platform bellowing orders. He was busy handing out assignments to latecomers.

"You over there! You're late," he yelled at an Elf. "Take it," he said, unfurling his fingers to send the information through the air. The numbers and letters reassembled in front of the Light Elf. "I'm sorry, not sorry," the Dwarf shrugged. "Next time, get your ass here on time. You take out that old Witch and I'll give you a harder target the next time. Think of her as an appetizer. A palate cleanser."

The Elf stormed out, grumbling but he took the coordinates with him.

Sal snorted and looked over who was left in front of him. "Everybody wants to bag the tough ones. Okay, who's next?"

"Ow! Who the hell did that?" A mountain Dwarf in the crowd held his elbow, a blister forming on the skin. His eyes narrowed as he looked around at the crowd. A tall female Light Elf stepped forward, small fireballs still dancing in the palm of her hand. Her long dark hair hung down to her waist, tucked behind her ears.

"Janine, of course. Always have to make a fucking entrance," snarled Sal. "Did you have to zing my brother? Sorry about that Marvin." Sal put his hand up to the side of his face, whispering loudly. "I'll be hearing about this for a month of Mondays."

"I can hear you and I'm telling Mom."

"Geez, grow a pair, Marvin," said Sal, rolling his eyes. "That's the real badass of the family. Mama can give you the willies with just a look," he said with a shudder. Sal clapped his hands together and ignored Marvin's protests. "Janine, I saved a good one for you. I had a feeling you'd show up and being the squeaky flaming wheel of painful fire that you are, I'd like to keep you happy. Here we go." Sal sent the coordinates tumbling across the room, spinning in a jumbled ball of letters and numbers, reassembling in front of Janine. "A forty-ish Witch in Raleigh, North Carolina hiding in plain sight. Two kids, looks like she has a human husband, and she works in IT for a local corporation. No one ever notices her. It *was* the perfect cover." He clapped his hands together in delight. "Boy, what a day! Imagine what we'll be able to do once this part is over."

Janine closed her hand to put out the fireballs,

reopening it to gather the coordinates into her palm. Her other hand rested on her bony hip. "Just what do you get out of this Sal?"

"Opportunity, my dear, that comes along sooner rather than later. If I had to wait for all of you to organize yourselves enough to pick off the agents, I'd be waiting for years. Some would go underground, maybe reunite and come back together." He swatted at the air, dismissively. "I don't have that kind of time. Okay, next! I have a fairly decent one. Middle aged Wizard and Witch out of Spokane. Middling trouble, I'd say."

Janine slipped out of the apartment, pulling her hoody up over her head as she headed for the elevator. She pushed the button, not making eye contact with the elderly couple pressed against the wall in the back. Once she made it to the lobby, she strode out the door and headed for the nearest subway entrance. She took the stairs down to the platform heading for Manhattan and walked halfway down the long stretch to a metal bench fastened to the wall. It was occupied by a Wizard with a knit cap pulled down low, slumped over in the seat, his forearms resting on his legs. Janine stood just to his right, scowling at a young man walking past her.

"What you looking at?" she snarled, making the man hurriedly look away. Everyone else did the same, keeping their distance. The man on the bench chuckled quietly as he opened his hand just enough to receive the tangled ball of numbers and letters. Janine opened her hand just enough to let the information slide from her to the Wizard's hand. "Eighth floor, apartment G. Better hurry. Sal's not wasting any time," she said. "Use the scorched earth approach and send a message that it's not worth low lying thugs time."

"Money will be in your account momentarily," the Wizard muttered.

"I'm off to the next auction. I'll let you know what I find." Janine leaned closer. "Once this is over, tell Lois this makes us even."

"You can go back to terrorizing the underworld," snorted the Wizard, "till you get caught again."

"Whatever," spit out Janine as the D train pulled into the station. "I can't believe humans ride these things," she said, as she pushed off the wall with the heel of her boot and headed back up the stairs.

CHAPTER TEN

Matthew Moss carefully laid out his clothes. He folded each item and slid them into the water-proof bag that matched the ground cover along Rock Creek Park. The sun had finally set, and a quarter moon hung in the sky. The only light was from the occasional streetlamp but most of the park sat in darkness. He knelt down, the cold air blowing across his bare back. He pushed aside the leaves on the ground and opened the lid to a metal box buried level with the ground.

The lid had barely opened before thick, wiry hair sprouted along his spine and tufts appeared on the backs of his hands. He squeezed his eyes shut at the first wave of a dull ache. His bones crunched and twisted, stretching his jaw out as fangs grew, protruding from his lips. Hands became large paws and legs grew, becoming more muscular. It wasn't long before the transformation was complete. The wolf sat back on his haunches and lifted his head, baying at what little there was of a moon.

Other calls answered him, and his ears twitched,

turning in different directions. The others were near and growing closer. He stayed in the shadows, watching a jogger run past him, unaware of how close she was to a shifter. He sniffed the air and smelled lavender mixed with vanilla, picking up a strain of the music from her phone. *Macklemore. Not bad taste.*

The runner got further down the path, passing under the light. The wolf could hear the others getting closer and watched, hoping she wouldn't linger in the area. She glanced back once, small lines of worry across her forehead, but kept running toward the far east side of the park. *Good. More humans and a police way station.*

A large yellow wolf came bounding out of the thicket of trees, closely followed by three more dark haired wolves, one with graying hair around its muzzle. The pack quickly assembled behind Matthew, pawing at the ground. Matthew snapped at them, growling and showing his teeth till they settled down.

Finally, their target came into view. A skinny Wizard in tight jeans with a windbreaker zipped up to his neck came shuffling through the park, continuously glancing over his shoulder. He rubbed at his nose nervously, jamming his hands into his coat pockets. Matthew waited till he was in just the right spot. Then he poked his large furry head up above where they were hidden and howled. The Wizard startled and slid out his wand from a pocket in his jeans, holding it up in front of him in the direction of the howl.

Other shifters answered the call from different directions filling the night air with barking and growling. The Wizard's eyes grew large and he turned in a tight circle. "What the fuck?" He tried to peer into the darkness, ducking down. "I don't have no quarrel with any of you. It was a job," he yelled. He spun small circles above his head, creating glowing yellow orbs that bobbed in the air. "Find them," he whispered, bringing the wand down in a quick motion. The lights zipped to their destinations, one of them hanging just above Matthew and his pack.

The other lights zigged and zagged through the trees till the park was dotted with lights.

The Wizard looked at the lights and his knees shook. "How... how... how..." He held up his wand, the tip bobbling and tried to stutter his way through a spell. "Mmmm-maddd dddoooogggsss disappear..." It wasn't enough to do much of anything, and the young Wizard knew it. He tried running, almost tripping over the loose shoelaces on his high top Converse sneakers but managed to make it to the next streetlight.

The wolves converged from every angle, jumping onto the path and taking their time. They slowly padded closer and closer to the Wizard, the orbs bouncing over them till the young magical was in a spotlight, ringed by large wolves. They were growling and baring their teeth, their heads hanging low between their shoulders. Matthew pushed to the front just in front of the Wizard. He stepped close enough to let the magical feel the steamy breath and feel the low rumbling growl pass through him.

"What do you want with me?" squeaked the Wizard.

In one swift motion Matthew raised a paw and a large grey wolf leapt at the Wizard, biting the back of his jacket and pulling him off his feet. The Wizard cried out, dropping his wand as they pulled him along the dirt at a run, his heels leaving a matching trail behind him. The orbs bounced along above them.

The pack stopped once they had gotten to the deepest part of the park where no one dared venture after sundown. Matthew barked and the grey wolf let go, letting the Wizard's head bounce against the hard, dirt. The orbs extinguished one at a time till they were covered in darkness once again.

Matthew stretched, turning his head to the left and the right as his body morphed back into human form. The other wolves made a circle around them, protecting the pair from view. Once the transformation was complete, he knelt down next to the magical and leaned a hand against his chest. Shadows fell along his lean, muscular body. "You get one opportunity. Just one. After that, I turn you over to my brethren. Understood?" asked Matthew, his eyes cold. "We know you poisoned one of us." Matthew pressed harder. "Don't deny it. That will make things worse. You were seen." Matthew leaned closer. "Tell us everything."

The words spilled out of the magical as if he couldn't say them fast enough. "I was hired off the dark web with a few others. The guy said we just had to paint a doorknob just ahead of the mark. It was easy money. We all got a baby jar full of the stuff. He said it can't harm humans or other magicals. Just..." He looked around at all the glowing eyes staring at him. "Just shifters." He swallowed hard, his face shiny with sweat. "Magic is supposed to come out in the open and tear things wide open." His eyes widened. "Poor choice of words," he muttered. "Everyone knowing about magic is a good thing. It can only help magicals.

Even your kind." An auburn-haired wolf behind the Wizard's head growled. "No offense."

"Who hired you?"

"Somebody called him Wolf something. Kind of ironic." He held his hands up in front of his face when one of the wolves started growling. "Okay, okay. Uh, Wolfstan. He was grinning from ear to ear. Said something about sowing chaos and spreading the opposition thin. That's all I know, I swear."

The Wizard squeezed his eyes shut. "Do it quick, have some pity on me." He lifted his chin as if he was trying to make it easier.

"You ever try to harm a shifter again, you won't hear or see us coming and they'll be able to bury you in several graves miles apart." Matthew felt something warm against his knee and looked down to see that there was a dark stain growing along the Wizard's leg. "I'll take that as your acknowledgment," said Matthew. "Listen carefully. Post on the dark web that the shifters have organized, and we are keeping watch for who would dare harm us. We're like a hairy Santa Clause with teeth. We're gonna make lists and check them twice. If you're on it, we will work as a tribe to make sure it doesn't happen again. You are the only magical who will get a second chance, if you post our warning."

The Wizard vigorously nodded his head. "Consider it done. I'll scare the shit out of them. Really lay it on."

"Tag Wolfman-one-two-three in the post."

"Got it." The Wizard was breathing hard still laying back against the dirt.

Matthew removed his hand and pulled him up by the

front of his shirt. "Get out of here. You have one hour to get it done. You'd better hurry."

The magical rose slowly, looking at all the wolves around him. He started to walk toward the closest exit but the wolves in front of him growled and he backed up again.

"Let him pass," said Matthew, a sly smile on his lips. The wolves stepped back just enough to let the Wizard pass, his legs brushing against their fur. He gradually picked up speed, walking faster till he was no longer near a streetlight and he started running, quickly disappearing in the distance.

"Still time for a run through the park," said Matthew, crouching. "Who's in?"

The wolves yipped and barked, pawing the ground. "That's what I thought. Who says we don't know how to have fun? Just give me a second."

There were the sounds of bones crunching as Matthew shifted back into a wolf. He lifted his head and howled before taking off at a run. The other wolves were right behind him, running through the park calling back and forth to each other. Two runners at the entrance to the park looked at each other and shook their heads, turning around to go back the way they had come.

CHAPTER ELEVEN

The old King of Oriceran stepped onto the private reserve and hesitated, listening. He heard the sounds of shifters calling to each other, waiting patiently for the one distinctive howl. "There it is," he said, smiling. At long last, he was near Lucius. He marched up the hill on Turner Underwood's old land and stood in the center of an open field. The old king stood up straight, dressed in his old battle gear and did his best imitation of howling, beating his fists against his leather armor. "Oooowww-woooooooo!" he cried out. "Ooooowwwwooooooo!"

It didn't take long for the ground to shake as the wolves came running from deep in the reserve and cresting at the hill. They pawed at the dirt, growling and snarling, their ears pinned back but the king held his ground. He lifted his fists high over his head and roared.

The wolves suddenly grew quiet and stepped back leaving a path for a weathered old Light Elf to march to the front. Lucius stood at the top of the hill in work boots, jeans and a green sweater. His long hair was pulled back in a braid. The king looked puzzled, staring at Lucius' outfit but a smile broke across his face and he reared his back, his belly shaking with laughter. Lucius came running down the hill, the pack moving easily alongside him. He stopped just a few yards short of the old king and stared at him, saying nothing.

Finally, the king spoke. "I always did say you had a knack for adapting to your circumstances."

Lucius didn't move at first, but the corners of his mouth began to turn up and he finally broke into laughter. "Turner Underwood insisted I stop wearing my old gear. How did you get away with it?"

"I outrank him. How are you, old friend? I've been searching for you for quite a long time."

A swirl of grey smoke appeared between them and in a blink, Turner Underwood was standing there, tapping his cane against the ground. His hand was firmly grasped around the silver eagle on the top. He took off his bowler and gave a slight bow to the king, his lips pressed together in frustration. He placed his hat back on his head with a sharp tap and waved his arms, the smoke clearing. "I told you I would make the introductions. No one was keeping you from him."

"I like to set my own schedule," said the king, with a wry smile. "Besides, you have more pressing business these days. Too many magicals are in need of your help. I have this matter in hand. Go rescue the masses."

"That matter is also in hand. I have recruited help from some unlikely sources."

The king raised his chin, looking down his nose at

Turner. "I can only begin to imagine. You are a very clever Fixer."

"Retired, emeritus," said Turner. "I have been replaced. Well, go on, tell him why we're all gathered here today."

The king let out an exasperated sigh. "I was about to when you made one of your glorious entrances." The king rubbed his face with his hand. "Where was I?"

Lucius stepped out from his pack and weaved his way around Turner, giving him a sidelong glance. "It's like you think I'll run amok," muttered Lucius.

"I can't imagine what gave me that impression," said Turner, getting out of the way as Lucius reached out for the king.

"Reunited at last and in a far better place," he said, grasping the king in a bear hug and pounding on his back.

"We have lived through heaven and hell and come back from worse to tell about it," said the king, with a laugh. He stepped back, holding on to Lucius' shoulders. "You look good, even in this outfit."

"If we can pause the bromance," said Turner, "and get on with the point of this meeting."

The king arched a brow but cleared his throat and let go of Lucius. "You and your kind, you're the answer to a very thorny problem. Your ability to shift from one type of being to a completely different one and regenerate every time. It's the answer and a way to stop Wolfstan Humphrey."

Lucius growled at the mention of Wolfstan. "What are you talking about?"

"It's your blood. It carried a magic, an energy that is very unique and very powerful. It's the last piece of a puzzle with a rare exception. Yours in particular, Lucius is the most powerful of all. A Light Elf who was made into a shifter who lived in the world in between. Your blood is the most powerful of all."

"You're speaking in riddles. First tell me what the question is."

"Wolfstan Humphrey has mutated an army of magicals into grotesque monsters to fight his battles. Innocents who were kidnapped and maimed. Harkin's machine..."

"The one that saved his friend."

"Yes, that's right. Think about how it works and think about the world in between and what it does. That dimension can hold a being's DNA in a static form. No one ages, no one ever finally dies. It's constantly regenerating the cells of every being in there."

Lucius' mouth dropped open and he slapped his forehead. "Like Harkin's machine but with a lot more force."

"A thousand times a thousand. The machine is similar to how the world in between operates but on a smaller scale. The only thing it lacks is enough raw energy. What supplies the world in between are the inhabitants. It's a symbiotic relationship where one feeds the other. But stay in the world in between long enough and our cells are transmuted permanently. You've probably noticed you transform into a wolf more easily than the others."

"No pain."

"No pain because your DNA has an added something. It runs through your blood. To a lesser degree, it runs through the humans who were changed into shifters by Sirius and his clan. The same quirk." He slapped a heavy hand on Lucius' shoulder as Turner watched patiently. "If you're willing," said the king, "your blood, and the blood of your kind can save them all and thwart Wolfstan Humphrey. Like I said, the missing piece of the puzzle."

"But you've been looking for me far longer."

"I've watched Harkin from inside that murky hell and I've had hundreds of years to piece everything together. I saw what Wolfstan was planning at the very beginning when no one else had noticed yet. I'm just sorry it took me so long to get out and then find you."

Turner raised his cane and waved it in the air. "Will you help, Lucius? Will you rally the shifters and let them help the magical world? It's a big ask, given how shifters have been treated."

"You have my word, my liege, my old friend. We will take on this challenge." Lucius raised his fist into the air. "Am I right?" he bellowed. The wolves raised their heads in unison, letting out a baleful cry that was heard that night for miles around. Pets grew restless pawing at their doors, whining to get out and birds took to the air, flying first in one direction and then another. Lucius smiled and looked at Turner and the king. "You have our word."

CHAPTER TWELVE

Ariana stood at the iron gates in front of the Kentucky estate. She raised her arms out into a V-shape, her long black coat flowing out behind her in the wind. In her right hand was a family heirloom. A wand made from a hickory tree grown on the property hundreds of years ago. "For all those who seek shelter will find a path. For all those who would cause harm will feel my wrath."

A crack of lightning could be heard in the dark starry night overhead. Uncle Felix stood next to her in another perfectly fitting suit, his hands on his hips, watching everything with an amused expression. "My dear, weren't you the one who made the deal with Mr. Humphrey that brought about this conundrum?"

Ariana tightened her grip around the wand and lowered her arms. She stared straight ahead as the gates opened under their own power. Witches and Wizards began streaming in, many of them holding the hands of small children. All of them carrying suitcases and boxes with a dazed expression saved for those fleeing for their lives.

"I wanted the Silver Griffins disabled. I never wanted our own kind slaughtered wholesale."

"Details can be so important, especially when asking a madman, don't you think? Especially one who has proven to be as clever and determined. Ah well, learning curves are a real bitch, aren't they?"

"I swear, dear Uncle if you don't shut the fuck up and prove yourself the slightest bit useful I will finally perfect that spell and turn you into a weasel." Her words were icy cold and for just a moment the smile slipped off her uncle's face. It reappeared a moment later, but he chose his words more judiciously.

"Fine, then a little bit of useful advice. Since they're here, treat them well. Very well. You may just find a few recruits to our particular lifestyle. Treat them badly, and they'll never forget, and they'll look for a reason to bring you down. Little do they know, you've already given them a really good one. You foolishly thought you could break up the Silver Griffins without consequences." Uncle Felix waved his wand, providing a soothing light for the refugees wandering down the driveway. "But mark my words, in one fashion or another they will reform and come back. In the meantime, Lois and her gal pal Patsy and all the rest will look for who helped Wolfstan Humphrey and they'll ask themselves a very important question."

Ariana sucked in her cheeks just a little, her jaw set.

"With all that lunatic had on his plate, why would he cause such trouble?" asked her uncle. "Oh, a bonus. Now that it's done, Wolfstan will want something for it. I know,

I know, you kicked him out. Do you think he will care? Watch your back and hope he dies. That would be the best outcome for you at this point." Uncle Felix turned to go, waving his wand to make a Witch's heavy suitcase a little lighter. He shook his head as she tried to thank him. "Dear, you could do that for yourself, you know. We allow magic here. The more the merrier. No need to play pack mule on our account. Oh, Ariana," he said, remembering something. "There was that other thing you asked Wolfstan. What was it? Kill Leira Berens. And now you want to play nice with her. You need to get better at your long game if you want to survive. Sirius was crazy, no denying that, but the magical bastard could generally see ten moves ahead."

"Until he couldn't." Ariana pointed her wand at her uncle's chest, making small circles with it, pushing the air slowly out of his lungs. "Never underestimate me, Uncle. I make mistakes. I'll admit that, unlike Sirius who now rots in Trevilsom. And I learn from them. And unlike you," she said jabbing her wand in the air making him gasp, grabbing at his throat. "I always have a plan B."

He tried to lift his wand just as she jabbed harder, knocking him backward into the wet grass. She released the spell and walked by him, smiling at the gaping Witches and Wizards still making their way onto the grounds. "Family spat," she said, softening her expression. "He's fine. Uncle Felix always lands on his feet. Right this way. We've made up beds for everyone and there's hot food waiting for you too. We protect our own kind, remember that," she said, hoping the strain didn't show on her face. *Wolfstan Humphrey has to die for so many reasons. Some mistakes are best kept hidden, forever.* She watched the parade of fallen agents and felt an ache of regret in her chest mixed with a small panic. *I will figure this out*, she thought, tapping her wand in her hand, *because I have to.*

The sun was just rising over the shifters' community center, but Lucius was still awake, looking over the shoulder of a slightly built man with tousled brown hair. He was holding his phone and slowly pushing the buttons. "Okay, let's try it again, Lucius. If I put in a radius of, say, five miles then every shifter who's joined the app will appear like a pinpoint on the map. See?"

"Barry, maybe you should let him push the buttons." A sandy haired heavyset man slurped from a mug of coffee. Barry glared at him, but Lucius was already reaching over his shoulder, grasping at the phone. Barry let it go even as he held up his middle finger by his waist. "Thanks Calvin," he muttered. Calvin shrugged and went back to slurping.

"Dammit, why do they make these buttons so small?"

"Not really any buttons." Barry pulled in his chin at the growl from Lucius. "Okay, not the point I suppose. How about you tell me what exactly you need, and I do all the work for you? Happy to serve," he said holding out his hands, cupped together just under the phone. He smiled cautiously at Lucius as the Light Elf let go of the iPhone and it dropped into Barry's waiting hands. "Okay, so we need as many shifters as possible to donate blood, right?"

Lucius grunted and Barry paused but nothing further came out.

"Okay, I'll take that as a yes. But we don't want everyone

showing up at once and we need different places. Plus, we need to be ready to take the blood, store the blood. All these details to make sure things run smoothly. So far, we've got team captains spread out over different regions made up of three counties apiece. Each of them is coordinating a mobile donation unit and each of those will store the blood and drive it to the sanctuary in Texas."

"That will be thousands of donations. Does Harkin need that much blood?"

"That's a great question, Lucius," said Barry as Calvin rolled his eyes standing over by the pink box of Voodoo Donuts.

"Oooh Gorilla Grape," he said, licking his fingers before picking it up.

Lucius noticed and flicked a pea sized fireball aimed at Calvin's head, knocking him back a step just as he was about to take a bite. "Don't lick your fingers, it's gross," said Lucius, surprising Barry.

"Where were we?" Lucius took up his position behind Barry again, towering over him.

"Yeah, where were we?" asked Barry, a smile growing across his face. "Right now, we have thousands on standby who've agreed to donate at a moment's notice. We just need word from Harkin or whoever is in charge and an amount and we start putting out the word through the app. If it's critical we also have magicals ready to transport by portal. We're ready to go, but first we need to figure out how to capture Wolfstan's army without killing them..." His words trailed off and he sucked in his bottom lip, holding very still. He could feel Lucius hot breath on the top of his head. Calvin was chewing donut and watching intently, his eyebrows raised.

Lucius let out a sigh. "Wolfstan has figured out how to make it difficult for us to defend ourselves. There's a reason he's one of the few to survive Trevilsom and get out alive."

Barry cleared his throat. "Yeah, well, we have Harkin. He did the same. And then there's you. You got out of the world in between. I'd say the odds are in our favor."

Lucius clamped a hand down on Barry's shoulder, shaking the smaller man's entire body. "Excellent point. You've done good work here. We will overcome this beast yet and prove victorious. The only question is how many will we lose before that day arrives?"

Calvin stopped mid-bite and closed his mouth, swallowing hard.

"Sir, we will run alongside you to the last of us."

"Same here," said Calvin, lifting his half-eaten donut slightly and nodding.

"Let's get the first batch started and sent to Harkin. Just a small supply. The battle is drawing near." Lucius took a step back and looked around the room at everyone working away on different projects. "Wolfstan Humphrey thinks he can tear apart the magical world. He's taken on all of us, but there's nothing like a common enemy to bring everyone to the table. He has no idea what he's unleashed, but he will. We will make sure of it."

CHAPTER THIRTEEN

The tall, elderly oak tree in the center of the Dark Forest shook as several leaves floated down to the forest floor. The thick, rough bark shimmered, and the Dryad emerged, pulling herself free and standing in the dappled light. She stood quietly, patiently waiting, feeling the movement of different animals. The vibration rolled under her feet, which were pressed against the soft, green moss crawling up over the roots. All of the large animals were moving in to the darker, dense parts of the forest, away from the edges of the Kingdom of Virgo or Oriceran or the mountain ranges where the Gnomes lived.

They moved in an orderly fashion. No creatures were stampeding or pushing past others.

"You really think this is necessary?" asked the Dryad without bothering to turn and look. The Gardener of the Dark Forest came up behind her and kissed her on her neck, the vines in his hair brushing across her back.

"You always were the only creature on Oriceran who could hear my approach," said the Gardener.

"You're avoiding my question. You've asked every living thing to draw away from the edges." She leaned her head back against the Gardener's muscled chest. "You're closing the Dark Forest. Have things become that dire?"

"I've always found it foolish to wait until the evidence is overwhelming and enough harm has been done that all can agree to take action. I don't need a consensus. Enough has already been done."

"But I've heard that the Light Elf's machine is finally successful. The shifter blood has worked, and they were able to transform a cow back to its original body. It's a reason to celebrate."

"It's a reason to have hope the Dark Forest may be open again someday, but that's all."

The Dryad watched as vines and trees began to fill in the edges of the forest, erasing well-worn paths. The only sunlight came from the top and what could pierce through the canopy. A fawn came trotting up to the Dryad and nuzzled against her. "The animals seem relieved. What about the magicals who live within the borders of the forest? Will they be allowed to remain?"

"Only a handful will find it possible to come and go. Jackson is one of them. He's always been a friend. But many will find themselves waking up in a field or next to the ocean with no idea how they got there. And no way to get back."

The Dryad walked in a slow circle around the Gardener, running a finger along his shoulders. "Your legend will only grow. Most are not sure you even exist." She arched a brow and looked at her mate. "I know that has some appeal to you."

"It appeals to me if it stops the slaughter. Magicals eventually ask too much and every hundred years or so I've had to push them back out of the forest. This is no different." The Gardener crossed his arms over his chest. "Before you ask, Perrom will be deep within the Forest, where he prefers these days. He may not even realize that it's closed."

The Dryad lifted her chin, smelling the breeze. "Rain is coming. That will be good. Drive everyone inside. By the time they emerge, the wards will be in place." She let out the breath she'd been holding in the center of her chest. "This will benefit every living thing in this forest, except for your son. He needs to come out among friends again."

"It won't matter till he's ready. And until then, we get on with our lives," said the Gardener with a deeper scowl than he normally showed.

"I know you check on him. I see you from time to time as I pass through the trees or an old oak or hickory will tell me."

"It's a very hard thing to know that sometimes we can love someone, but we can't save them. We can only watch and hope..."

"And maybe set a good example. A reason to come back out."

"Ossonia is the only reason he's willing to consider at the moment."

The Dryad winced at the mention of the Light Elf's name. "The heart can heal from anything. We both know that better than most. I know why you started this forest in the first place."

"We agreed to never speak of our first born. Not ever."

"Well, times change and sometimes we have to do

something unbearable for the right reasons." The Dryad looked off into the distance. "So much time has gone by and I've had time to think about it. I think we were wrong to let Luca become just a memory shared by two. He deserved better than that. Perrom doesn't even know..."

"And finding out may make him angrier. He may see it as a lie or a betrayal."

The Dryad stepped back, blending with the tree behind her momentarily, as it wrapped its trunk around her like a comforting hug. "We will revisit this. When the time is right." She faded into the tree leaving the Gardener standing alone in the copse of trees. "Luca," whispered the Gardener pressing his fist to his chest. The vines through his hair turned a deep navy blue, warming again to green as he shook his head. "Some things are meant to stay buried, even if we never got the chance to do just that," he said, marching off into the forest, letting out a roar that unsettled the birds overhead.

CHAPTER FOURTEEN

"I don't know about this." Harkin looked up at the red tracks of the roller coaster, stretching three hundred and five feet above his head. It was simplistic in design with no loops and only one very tall arch that had the rider looking straight up at the sky, and then plummeting, suddenly looking at the approaching ground. "Why do they call it the Intimidator?"

Correk furrowed his brow, looking at his father. "You're worried about riding a roller coaster? You survived Wolfstan Humphrey as a bunkmate in Trevilsom Prison. This is a ride that's meant to be fun. Perfectly safe."

Harkin leaned back and took another look, not saying anything, his long braid swishing across his broad back. "Humans put this together, right?"

Correk let out a sigh. "I see where you're going with this one. It'll be fine. Look, we're supposed to be on a father and son outing. Leira's orders." Correk shrugged and held up his hands. "I know, I know. But she has these kinds of memories with her mother and grandmother, she wanted us to make a few too."

"We came to the... what did you call this?"

"Amusement park."

Two teenage boys wearing jeans that had slid down enough to show off the top of neon colored underwear slunk by them. The skinnier of the two looked the Light Elves up and down. "Look, Thor brought his dad to Kings Dominion. Where's your hammer, dude?" snorted the kid, elbowing his friend.

They jostled each other, laughing as they made their way to the line for the ride.

"Who's Thor?" asked Harkin. "Do we know a Thor? Was he a carpenter on Oriceran?"

Correk smiled gently at his father. "Dad, it's not important. Yumfuck can fill you in later. He's kind of the resident expert on movies, old and new. Look, if you don't want to get on the ride, we can go find something else that's not quite so... scary," he said, trying not to let his smile grow. "It has occurred to you that if there's a problem we can actually use magic. Like real magic."

"There's no magic that can make an Elf fly. Hell, Witches don't even fly." He tapped the side of his head with a calloused finger. "What is that spell for quickly putting things back in order."

"Okay, we're going to another ride," said Correk, walking away from the Intimidator.

But Harkin grabbed his arm. "No wait, I can do this. It'll be... fun. An adventure. What did Leira call this whole thing?"

Correk arched a brow. "A bonding experience. Okay, I'll

go on it with you but if you cry, I'm buying the picture they take and I'm framing it."

Harkin finally let out a deep, loud laugh, startling a flock of teenage girls. He clapped Correk hard on the back, leaving his arm resting around his son's shoulders. "Okay, I'm in," he said as they walked toward the line. "Besides, I think I remember that spell." An idea occurred to him and his face lit up. "Hey, I'm even here with the Fixer. Things really go south, you're bound to know something."

"Way to work it out, Dad. I think there was a compliment in there somewhere," said Correk, chuckling. They got to the back of the line, not too far behind the two teenage boys, still trading jokes and poking each other.

"You used to be like that with Perrom," said Harkin, wistfully.

"Not even for a day." Correk crossed his arms over his chest.

"For quite a few years. I had to go speak to teachers more than once because you and Perrom had tried some spell to make the class laugh. You always thought you'd get away with it."

"Who says I didn't at least some of the time?"

Harkin laughed, the lines around his eyes deepening. "Good point." He cleared his throat, looking down at his boots and then up at the top of the ride.

"What is it? Are we confessing things already?" asked Correk. He shook his head in disbelief. "Leira will love knowing she was right. These things do work."

Harkin rolled his eyes. "I was just going to say that I'm glad you found Leira. She's been good for you. All that trouble with me really changed you. She's managed to loosen you up a bit."

"She likes to say she's a doctor because she removed the stick out of my ass," said Correk, dryly.

Harkin slapped his knee and laughed. "See what I mean? She's a good mate. You'll have a lot of fine Elves."

Correk's eyes widened and his face grew warm. "I don't know about a lot..."

"Time will tell," said Harkin, pursing his lips and glancing one more time up at the top of the enormous arch as they stepped up to the front of the line. Correk looked over at his father as the people in front of them walked to their seat. "You're practicing a spell, aren't you?"

Harkin ignored him as the man running the ride opened the gate and pointed to the seat in the front. "Oh look, we're in the front. The best view," said Harkin.

Correk's brow furrowed as he looked at his father, but he didn't say anything. They were buckled in and the bar was pulled down in front and locked into place. "All hands and feet stay inside the ride. Everything in your pockets secured? Okay, good," said the park employee, not waiting for an answer.

"Harkin, uh, when you're in the front seat..."

Correk was cut off by the yelling and cheering from the teenagers a few rows back and the ride starting with a *click, click, click*. "So far so good," said Harkin, gripping the metal bar across their laps. The chain of brightly orange painted cars whizzed around flat loops, jerking Correk and Harkin first to the left and then to the right several times until they approached the main event. The tall arch.

The cars began to climb, pushing the two Light Elves

back against the seat and looking straight up at the puffy clouds in the sky. "I've walked around an invisible castle," said Harkin. "This should be easier." The carts continued to climb until they reached the top and became level again.

Correk moved his hand closer to his father's, which was tightly gripping the bar. "Here we go, Dad. Hang on." *Click, click, click.* The car came to the edge... and stopped cold.

Harkin looked around at the sights. "Is this part of it? I have to say, this is a pleasant surprise. I didn't expect the chance to see the view."

Correk licked his upper lip and took in a deep breath slowly, letting it out. "Uh, nope, this isn't a typical part of the ride."

Murmurs could be heard behind them, the volume gradually increasing as seconds ticked by. One of the teenage boys was rising out of his seat yelling, "I can see my house. I can see the Potomac. I can see Fredericksburg."

"Shut the hell up!" yelled a burly man in a Motorhead t-shirt with a bushy moustache and dark blue tattoos down one arm.

Harkin's eyebrows slowly went up and he seemed to be making himself loosen his grip on the bar as he turned to his son. "Something's gone wrong, hasn't it?"

"It would appear that way," said Correk, glancing over the side at the precipitous drop equal to twenty-one stories that was right in front of them. "The troll would love this," he muttered.

Nearby speakers crackled with sound and the voice of the park employee came over the loudspeaker. "Sit tight folks. Just a minor glitch." His voice cracked for a moment, but he kept speaking. "Nothing to be concerned about. The cars in front of you are stuck below so we need to hold you right here. Shouldn't be too long. Please keep all arms and legs inside your car and stay seated." The loudspeaker crackled again and went silent.

"I suppose it's good that it's not our cars," said Harkin, looking straight ahead.

"Imagine you're walking into the library in Oriceran and the only things that are visible are the book stacks," said Correk.

"I think I've realized something important. I trust magical floors more than human engineering." Harkin sucked in his cheeks and then blew them out. "I feel queasy."

"That's an unfortunate turn of events. Try and take small breaths. Human engineering is amazing, you know that. It's humans who have made a lot of the electronic parts that make your beloved machine work."

"That damnable machine," said Harkin, gripping the bar harder again, trying to breathe in. "We have to duplicate it into a hundred of them at least and get it all right without any time. What if I do something wrong and... and..."

"Dad, it's not all on you this time. You have help with Lily and we can find others. It's going to take a lot of us to accomplish any progress." Correk drummed his fingers on the bar, trying to come up with something else. "Have I mentioned that Yumfuck is building something in his room but won't show anyone but Leira's mother so far? Not much of a subject, okay. I can do better."

Harkin closed his eyes, his complexion growing a little paler.

Correk shifted in his seat toward Harkin. "I'm sorry I gave up on you."

Harkin's eyes popped open. "What? Why would you say that? I gave you very good reasons."

"In some ways you did, in other ways you didn't. You lost the love of your life and I didn't understand."

"You lost your mother."

"True, but it's different. If I lost Leira I don't know that I could go on... And I think of Perrom."

"It's a hard thing for a Light Elf to lose their life partner. It's like part of our magic is ripped away from us." Harkin let his shoulders drop. "It turns out your mother was the brains of the operation. Not a surprise. Without her, I was always trying to figure out how to fix things. In the end, what I learned is sometimes it's best to leave things alone. I learned that a little too late."

"Enough people have reminded you that Peyton would have died without your intervention."

"That may have been a better fate than decades of torture. But it's not what I was talking about." Harkin looked down at his lap. "It was suggested to me, even before Peyton, that if I stepped back from your life you would be chosen for the royal court. I didn't want to get in your way so I tried to fix things..."

Correk's eyes widened in horror and a shudder passed down his spine. "Who would say such a..." The words trailed off.

"It was the Light Elf, Fraekin. Wolfstan knew what he was doing when he chose to murder him. I should have never listened."

The loudspeakers crackled again, and the same voice

erupted suddenly into the air. "Just a few more minutes, folks. Hang tight." The sound abruptly cut off as people began to protest louder and the teenage boys continued to make jokes.

"Alfie, you can climb down the scaffolding on that side," yelled a boy with curly blonde hair. "I'll follow the tracks going backward."

"If you don't shut the fuck up, I'm going to climb out of this car," said the muscled man in the Motorheads t-shirt. His face was beet red.

"You better do something, Fixer. From the looks of things, we're the only magicals on this ride," said Harkin, grimacing. "The humans are about to revolt."

Correk whispered into his closed hand and opened his fingers, releasing a fine gold dust that the wind picked up and blew over their heads. "Like a magical sedative," said Correk. The protests quieted down, and the other passengers began to look around at the view.

"Much better," said Harkin. "I'm really proud of you for taking on the mantle of becoming the Fixer. You proved just how wise Turner Underwood is."

Correk smiled and leaned toward his father. He wasn't going to let his father change the subject. "I still owe you an apology. I could have asked questions all those years ago. Any questions. Instead I assumed the worst. I thought you were leaving me because you didn't want the responsibility and were only thinking of yourself. I can see now that is one thing you've never actually done. Every move, even the ones that have failed were about trying to help someone else."

"I suppose that's a family trait of the male elves for us.

We don't talk enough. Your mother was the one who could take one look at me and know I was stewing."

"Leira's a lot like that. She sees right through me and reflects back this better version of myself." A bird sailed over everyone's head close enough for riders to count the feathers, eliciting ooooohs and aaaaahhhhs. Everyone was in a magical drunken haze.

"I lost sight of something your mother was always saying," said Harkin. "A grateful Light Elf can never lose their way. I was so busy staring at what I lost, I forgot about who I still had and ended up losing you too."

"I'm here now and this time I'm not going anywhere and I'm not going to let you push me away."

"I won't repeat that mistake again. I want to be a part of this family. Even Mara and Yumfuck and Eireka and Don. It's like I got everything back tenfold."

The wind picked up rustling Correk's jacket and rocking the car slightly. He saw his father's eyes widen again. "Let's pick up one of my mother's traditions right now. Let's figure out what we can be grateful for. I'll start and list Leira and Yumfuck and... you."

"That's a better way to honor her memory than I've managed in far too long. Alright, I'm grateful for you and Leira and the troll and finally helping Peyton. Maybe even fixing the machine to help others. I'm grateful for Lily." He shook his head. "She's amazing. I've never met a Witch like her."

"And very young," said Correk, arching a brow, "for an Elf hundreds of years old."

"Maybe..."

The loudspeaker came on again as the cars gently

rocked forward for a click. "Okay, we're ready to go. Hang on everyone! We will finally finish up this ride. Coupons will be waiting for you at the bottom as you exit the ride. Thank you for your patience." He barely had the last words out before the carts started to tip over the edge. One by one, speeding toward the bottom. Correk let out a whoop, his arms raised over his head. The camera had flashed as they went over the front. Harkin's mouth was open in a round 'o' followed by a large grin.

They came to the bottom and zipped around to the left, sliding to one side as the car came down the stretch, gradually coming to a stop. Harkin and Correk were laughing as the bar clicked loose and they pushed it up, making their way back onto the platform.

"I think that was better than any magic I know," said Harkin, still laughing. He swayed slightly on his feet and Correk laughed, putting his arm around his father, guiding him toward the exit. The two teenage boys, still under the influence of the spell, passed them laughing and pushing each other.

"That was the best ride of my life!"

"Let's ride it again!'

"We have to get that picture."

Correk looked at Harkin. "They're right. We have to get that picture. At least two of them." They headed for the photo booth and stood in line. "You know, Dad. This was a lot of fun. We will have to listen to Leira more often."

"You are a wise Light Elf, my son." He leaned closer, watching the lazy grins on the other riders waiting around them. "Do you need to remove that spell?"

"No, it'll wear off by itself. Let them enjoy it. The good

feelings they have will become a permanent part of their memories."

"I know how they feel," said Harkin, looking around, a loopy smile on his face. Correk watched his father and blinked his eyes a few times. "Yeah, me too," he whispered, smiling.

CHAPTER FIFTEEN

Samuel was already sitting on the bench, his face tilted up toward the last warmth of the sun for the day. Yumfuck saw him from a distance and wove his way around bushes and near trees to avoid the stares of some late afternoon walkers. The weather was a perfect seventy-two degrees, and everyone was outside.

An older woman adjusted the cashmere scarf around her neck as a silver bracelet slid off her wrist. She bent down to pick it up in time to see Yumfuck cut across the path. The troll gave her a wave and a smile with all his pointy teeth on display.

"Oh," she murmured, standing back up and sliding the bracelet back on her wrist. "Phil was right. I do need glasses. I could swear that squirrel waved at me," she muttered, stepping aside for a bike to roll past her.

The troll came up behind the bench and walked underneath, hiding behind Samuel's shoes, still partially under the bench. He waited till the path was clear and finally came out, tugging on Samuel's pant leg. "I made it!"

Samuel broke into a smile, lowering his chin. "I knew you would. Or at least I hoped so. Always makes my day brighter. Do you need a hand up?" asked Samuel, bending down with his hand outstretched.

Yumfuck shrugged but jumped on board anyway as Samuel lifted his hand. The troll jumped onto Samuel's leg and took a seat, settling back against a soft cashmere cardigan.

"Weather's starting to change," said Samuel. "I can smell it in the air. This is one of the only times I feel a pang of regret about losing my sight. I can't see the leaves change. Ah well, have to focus on what I do still have." Samuel lifted his cane slightly into the air. "Hell, what I've gained lately. New friends, new adventures."

The troll stood up. "Speaking of new adventures. I have a good one in mind for today. Portia and George are celebrating the Autumnal Equinox. It's a big deal for Witches and Wizards and they sent me here specifically to ask you to join in the festivities."

"Something else to put on my gratitude list. I'll put it on my calendar."

The troll let out a whistle. "Well... that won't be necessary. I was supposed to tell you a while ago and it slipped my mind. Lots going on. It's kind of today. Kind of right now." Yumfuck threw his tiny arms over his head and let out a whoop. "Hurray!"

Samuel laughed, the wrinkles deepening in his face. "Way to pivot, my tiny furry friend. Will Nibbler be there too?"

"He's back on Oriceran with Jackson, but he'll be back soon. I have a plan to be discussed at a later date." The troll jumped down to the bench as Samuel slowly rose, leaning on his cane.

"Still a little sore from that rumble we had," said Samuel. "I think I held my own pretty well."

"You did better than pretty well." Yumfuck made his way down to the ground, pulling on his friend's pant leg to turn him toward the magical townhouse on N Street.

Samuel suddenly stopped in the middle of the sidewalk. "I don't have anything to contribute to the party," he said, his brow furrowing with worry. "You're gonna have to help me out with this one. Let me know if we pass a flower stand. My momma would tan my hide if she knew I went to someone's house empty handed."

"I am at your service at all times. We're buddies. *O Captain, my Captain,*" said the troll as they started to walk again. "*Rise up and hear the bells.*"

Samuel chuckled, moving his cane back and forth across the sidewalk in an arch as they walked. "Isn't that about a beloved *fallen* leader?"

"Okay, how about, *Come wake me up. Come any hour of night...*"

"Ah, Robert Francis. Much better. My favorite line is, *Tell me the walking is superb. Not only tell me but persuade me. You know I'm not too hard persuaded.* You've been doing more than just watching TV. Impressive."

"I'm very deep," said the troll. "Layer after layer," he said, rubbing his furry belly.

"Trolls are some of the most clever creatures on two planets. I have a theory that all those calories are to supply an amazing brain."

Yumfuck straightened up, puffing out his chest as they

waited at a light. "Samuel, you and I are gonna be buddies for a good long time. You really see us."

"Well, that's what friend's do. We see all the good parts of a being and promote those, shine em up good till they glow. It's an interesting thing," he said as they started to cross the street. "We tend to find what we look for and don't always think to stop and review the question we started with."

The troll gently pulled on Samuel's pant leg. "Flower shop two stores down."

"Thank you, friend."

"Anytime, buddy."

CHAPTER SIXTEEN

Samuel and Yumfuck finally arrived at the back gate, Samuel was holding a bouquet of red zinnias. Yumfuck scurried up and over the top of the gate. "Shouldn't we knock?" asked Samuel, but the troll was already in motion. He jumped down onto the lock and deftly moved the bolt with his feet, dancing across the thin metal bar. "Cowabunga!" he yelled, springing up and striking a superhero pose in mid-air before grabbing onto the gate with one paw and swinging outward.

"Samuel!" Marcy clapped her hands together and Emmett put down the plate of hamburger patties next to the grill. He walked over to Samuel and offered his arm. "You made it," he said. "My arm is just to your left. How about we cruise by the bar for a cocktail first. We have Bloody Mary's with a homemade secret sauce or some very fine Scotch or even a beer. Whatever you fancy."

Samuel's eyebrows went up as his dimples appeared. "Sounds perfect. This is gonna be my kind of party," he said, sliding his hand into the crook of Emmett's arm. "I wasn't sure what to expect because, you know, you folks being magical."

"Can I take those flowers from you?" asked Portia, waiting for Samuel to hold them out.

"These are for you. Thank you for inviting me."

"We consider you a member of our band now," yelled George from the wooden fire escape as he came down carrying a bag of ice.

"That's right," said Marcy, as the troll dropped down from the gate and quickly made his way across the grass and up, onto the picnic table. "Olives!" He quickly stuck an olive on each claw, just as quickly biting them off.

"Save a few for the rest of us," said George, setting down the ice and popping a green olive in his mouth. "Best part of a martini."

"I'll try one of those Bloody Marys," said Samuel. "I can never pass up a secret sauce. You people sound practically giddy this afternoon. Everybody already on their second round? Thank you," he said, taking the cold glass and trying a sip. "Oooh, that is good."

Portia came over and wrapped Samuel's free hand around her arm, leading him to a chair. "Samuel, you are here on a very special day for magicals in this world," she said, helping him sit and taking the chair next to him. "Two of them are the spring and fall equinoxes. On those two particular days the magic increases just for a while and something wonderful happens."

Marcy spun in a circle in the center of the yard. "Once the sun sets, we can be young again for just the night."

George winked at Portia who leaned closer to Samuel. "It takes a certain spell that's passed down through

Wizarding families. You have to be of a certain skill level but..."

"You could join us," said Emmett. "Just for this one night, we can all be young again."

"Are you in?" asked Portia.

"You'd be our first human to try it out." George fired up the grill, waving to Emmett to cart over the plate of hot dogs. Two were already missing and the troll was happily laying on his back on the table, his cheeks full, still chewing. "Price of doing business, I suppose," said Emmett with a shrug.

Samuel sat back in the chair, still holding on to his cane. He opened and closed his mouth before saying anything.

"Are you in?" asked Portia. "It's okay if you don't want to..."

"It's not that." Samuel interrupted her, waving his hands. "It's just that my first thought was about something I want even more. I don't know."

"Well, tell us and if we can, we'll do it. We've heard about how you helped those trolls and the price you paid." Portia patted him on the shoulder.

"I want to be able to see again," Samuel blurted. "Even if it's only for one night. I want to see the stars. I want to see the color of a leaf turning red. I want to see Yumfuck's face." A tear was slowly rolling down his cheek.

The troll stopped chewing and swallowed the remaining bite, despite its size. He wiped off his mouth on the tablecloth leaving a small grease stain but stayed where he was.

"I'm not sure that would happen," said Portia, quietly, glancing up at George, her eyes shining. "It might, simply because old knees are restored, and backs become strong. But I can't say with any certainty if old wounds would repair. We're all willing to try, if you want to give it a go."

Samuel pressed two fingers to his lips, blinking away tears that were clinging to his long dark lashes. "Even for a chance, I'm more than willing to try."

Emmett put his arm around Marcy as she laid her head on his shoulder. "It's almost dark and time to start. Portia, do you have your wand ready? You want to do the honors?"

Portia pulled out a wand made of cherry blossom wood. A rare thing indeed. "Everyone get in a circle around Samuel," she said as they made their way into a close circle with Samuel sitting in the middle. "What once was, will be again," said Portia, circling her wand in the air. "What is now, returns." She pulled a pinch of dried candyleaf and blew it into the air. "Under cover of darkness, amidst the light, bring back our youth, for just this one night."

A string of gold light emerged from the tip of Portia's wand and floated through the air, seeking out everyone in the circle. It wove in and out, in front and behind, leaving a trail everywhere it went. As the light completed its fourth pass, it suddenly turned toward the center of the circle, winding its way up Samuel's feet, creating a beehive of light around him as it got to the tip of his head.

The entire interior of the circle was aglow as a wind picked up that was isolated to just within the small circumference. Grey hair began to turn blonde and brunette again or even grow back on balding heads. Wrinkles disappeared and backs were straighter, and skin took on a dewy sheen. Emmett's waistline slimmed till he had to gather up the front of his pants to keep them from sliding down. Elijah held up his hands to show the taut skin.

Samuel who was in the center of the light grew younger, but his eyes remained cloudy. That is, until Portia waved her wand one more time, hoping for a little extra magic that she ended with the word, "Please."

Samuel's mouth dropped open as the light sought him out, swirling around his head, hiding his features. The others leaned in, anxious to see what was happening as the light abruptly turned to dust and blew off into the night, leaving them in the dimming twilight. Samuel took in a sharp gasp and his hands slowly rose up near his face, his fingers spread wide. The white cane that was always with him rolled to the ground. He blinked again as Marcy elbowed Emmett. "The lights," she whispered.

"Oh yeah." Emmett ran to the side of the building and threw a switch. Strings of lights that crossed the backyard lit up, illuminating everything. Samuel's eyes were clear and as he blinked, everything came into sharp focus. Tears streaked his face as he turned in a circle, his arms outstretched. Finally, he stopped and went over to Portia, wrapping her face in his hands. "You must be Portia. I'm right, aren't I?" He didn't wait for an answer before he was onto the next person. "And George! You're exactly as I picture."

"I'm Elijah, and it's nice to meet you all over again," he said, laughing, his hand pressed to his belly. Emmett came and stood next to Marcy and held out their arms to engulf Samuel.

"Wait! Where is he? Where is my friend?" Samuel spun

around, peering into the shadows in between the twinkling lights. "Yumfuck, where are you?"

The small, five inch troll strode into the center of the yard, just beneath where the twinkling lights crossed and stood up straight, his little paws on his hips. "Samuel, here I am. Can you see me?"

Samuel walked slowly over to the troll and knelt down in front of him, holding out his hand. Yumfuck eagerly climbed into his palm and waited patiently as Samuel lifted him up to where they were looking each other in the eye. "I can see all of you," whispered Samuel. "Your beautiful green fur on the top of your head and your brilliant blue eyes. You are as dashing as I expected, and then some."

Yumfuck put his tiny paws on either side of Samuel's nose and leaned in to give him a kiss. He backed up and said, "Thank you, my friend."

"They're here!" said Portia, looking up into the air.

"Oh, this is one of my favorite parts," gasped Marcy, clasping her hands to her chest.

Hundreds of fireflies poured over the fence and scattered into the air like glowing embers. They darted around the yard overhead, seemingly without direction.

Samuel put Yumfuck on his shoulder and stood up, his head tilted back. "Lightning bugs, and so many of them."

"Wait till you see what they do," said Elijah. "We are not the only ones who are celebrating the autumnal equinox and growing younger for just a little while.

The fireflies danced around, gathering closer together until it became clearer that they were forming letters in the night sky.

To our good friends on N Street. I hope our missive finds you well. Raise a glass for us. Jane and Larry.

The letters broke apart as the fireflies scattered, still hovering nearby, flying back and forth.

"Now it's our turn," said George, rubbing his hands together. "What do we want to say and who do we send it to?"

"It has to be Pauline and Winston. There will be dozens of Witches and Wizards gathered over there tonight," said Portia. "How about, peace and blessings on all the days ahead?"

"Perfect," said Marcy, as the others nodded. Portia raised her wand and moved it through the air like she was playing a piano. The fireflies responded, blinking on and off as they gathered in a glowing cloud and poured back over the fence.

Samuel continued to watch in amazement as he moved around the yard, trying to take in everything. "The leaves are starting to change! I didn't miss it." Yumfuck reached up and pulled down a leaf that was green with a deep golden around the edges and handed it to Samuel. "A keepsake," he said. "You can press it in a book."

"Here comes some more." Elijah pointed as another flood of fireflies approached from a different direction, winding through the buildings and over the fence. Everyone waited expectantly as they swirled in different directions before forming letters.

We survived another year around the sun. And saved you a piece of pie. Visit soon. All the love, The Bradleys.

"These go on all night," said Marcy, coming to stand

next to Samuel. "It meant more before texting," she laughed, "but it's tradition and so much fun."

"Just wait till everyone's had a few. Then the jokes start," said George.

"That was amazing," said Samuel, stretching his arms over his head. "I feel like I could lift something big over my head. I forgot what it felt like to move, and nothing aches."

"Was? The night's entertainment is just beginning. Crank up the music, Emmett," said George, as he grabbed his wife around the waist and twirled her across the grass.

"Can I have this boogie?" asked Marcy, holding out her hand to Samuel. "You'll have to forgive our dance styles, or admire them, either one. We're hundreds and hundreds of years old and we each have a favorite era."

"No one's really into classical, though," observed Elijah, clicking his heels. "Can only do that on the equinox," he said, breaking into the Charleston.

Samuel grasped Marcy's hand tighter. "Do you know how to jitterbug?"

"Do I ever!" she exclaimed.

They twirled round and round, their feet moving in fast, short steps, the troll bouncing and cackling on Samuel's shoulder. Samuel put his hand behind his back and Marcy grabbed it, as they both spun in opposite directions, coming back out facing each other. "That one's called the pretzel."

The dancing went on for most of the night, interrupted by passing notes from blinking fireflies and burgers from the grill washed down with Bloody Mary's and a secret sauce. It wouldn't be till close to sunrise that they began to slow down, their years slowly piling back onto their bones.

The gradual purple and yellow light that was spreading across the East grew dimmer for Samuel as his eyes slowly clouded over again. He stood frozen in one place, watching the light for as long as he could before it went out with a blink and was gone.

"Are you okay?" Yumfuck leaned over and whispered in his ear, still perched on his shoulder. He yawned, stretching his tiny mouth, all of his pointy teeth showing.

"Oh, I'm better than okay. I got to see the leaves changing and fireflies blinking, and I got to dance again without worrying about a hip. This has been one of the best nights of my life. There will never be enough words to say thank you."

"Then just come back in the spring and do it all again with us." Portia placed his cane in Samuel's hand and then wrapped her arms around him, hugging him tight. "You're one of our merry band now and forever."

"Like I was saying, there's so much more to be grateful for if you just remember, and I will always remember this night."

CHAPTER SEVENTEEN

The beefy Wizard in the jean jacket with the arms cut off looked confused. "We're looking for the concert," he said to the woman in the ticket window at the Agora Theatre on Euclid Avenue in Cleveland, Ohio. "The concierge at our hotel gave us directions to this place." He looked up and stepped back to gaze at the marquee again. Behind him were a dozen other Wizards with long hair and bears wearing similar jackets that all had Sons of Wizardry embroidered on the back with a skull and roses.

"That's right," said the young woman, bobbing her head. "They've been expecting you."

"Expecting us? How could you know we were coming?" He turned and looked at his friends who shrugged and crossed their beefy tattooed arms over their chests. A line of shiny Harley motorcycles were lined up along the curb behind them.

"Uh huh," said the woman, barely paying attention anymore, glancing at the long line forming behind the men. "Go down the alley and take the first side door." She jabbed her finger to the left, snapping gum in her mouth. "You'd better hurry," she said, tapping the watch on her wrist. "You're already late. Can you step aside so I can help everyone in line?"

"What about our tickets?"

"Tsk." The woman rolled her eyes, pushing her bangs out of her eyes. "You don't need tickets. Harry knows to just let you in. Don't worry, you'll be able to see the show from your positions. Now go! Hurry!" She batted her hands toward the man towering over her. "Go on."

He pulled his chin back, incredulous and turned around to his waiting friends. "I guess we go to the side door. Did one of you win a contest and not tell us? How are we getting to go backstage for Abba?"

"Hey, Bennie, if this is the Abba concert, why does the marquee say, Potty Mouth? That's not an Abba song. It sounds more like a comment."

"Dude, I tried reasoning with the high schooler, but she insisted and said we don't need tickets."

"You better be right," said a Wizard who was as wide as he was tall, with a red bandana tied around his head. "I was promised tenth row seats to see Abba, and I paid dearly for them. Susan was not happy when she found out I borrowed from our vacation fund for Disney."

"Yeah, borrow," snorted another biker.

Bennie got to the side door first and pounded on it. "Hey, we're here."

"Is that necessary? They'll think it's a raid with you knocking like that."

"I want to get to our seats, Joey and there's not a lot of

time left. I've been looking forward to *Take a Chance on Me* live for months."

The door opened and a skinny young man with purple hair wearing a shiny red shirt with billowing sleeves peeked out, looking the dozen Wizards up and down. "Man, they were not kidding. You guys are perfect. Come on," he said, waving over his shoulder as they filed in behind him. The noise from the crowd was already loud and just getting louder.

"Huh," said Joey, "that's a lot of enthusiasm for a night of *Dancing Queen*."

The young man laughed and turned around to give them a wink and point a finger. "Good one. I may have to steal that line."

"Good one?"

"You're all entitled to one free beer an hour and dinner, but that's not the great deal you might think, I'm telling you," he said, walking them toward a door that was getting closer to the rising noise. "I'll settle up with you at the end of the night. Everyone Venmo? Great." He opened the door and held out his hand. "Time to go to work," he said, pushing them into the concert hall. "If it were me, I'd split up and put two of you in six different places. I mean, those kids all look underfed and sleepy but get the music cranked up and they get very hard to handle."

"Hey Bennie, he thinks we're the muscle," said the tallest biker with a shiny bald head.

"Yeah, I'm catching on to that."

"Where the hell are we?" asked Joey.

"Didn't they tell you?" asked the manager, rolling his eyes. "Why do they always leave the details to me? You're at a Potty Mouth concert. Hottest new punk rock band in the Mid-West. Careful around the mosh pit. Lots of broken noses and ribs. Usual stuff. I gotta go see about the lights. They're about to start." He was talking a mile a minute, making it difficult for Bennie or anyone else to interrupt him. It wasn't helping that the volume was just getting louder in the room and Bennie had to shout to be heard.

"But where's Abba?" he shouted. The manager didn't hear him and was already making his way back through the door, slipping out and letting it shut behind him.

Someone threw a beer bottle at the stage and screamed, "Where are you, bitches?"

"Are we supposed to do something about that?" asked one of the Wizards.

"No, numbskull," said Bennie, exasperated. "We're not really security. Come on, let's find a way out of here."

Suddenly, the lights went up on the stage and three girls walked on stage. None of them were much over five feet tall and each of them had a different neon hair color. Two of them picked up guitars and the third sat behind a drum set. Without an introduction or even making eye contact with the crowd they started playing, screaming into the microphones and whipping their heads up and down.

"Holy shit!" yelled Bennie, but no one could hear him. All of the bikers put their hands over their ears and were moving their mouths, yelling something but it was too loud.

The mosh pit sprang up immediately and grew out toward the bikers. Someone occasionally climbed on the nearest shoulders to get to the top and throw themselves back, surfing along the top for a stretch, before being sucked under by a human tide of outstretched hands.

"Hey! Hey! Hey!" Joey windmilled his arms as the crowd reached out to grab him, lifting the large biker as if he were weightless and bouncing him along the top. Joey could be seen still screaming something, his eyes wide as Bennie and a few others tried to wade into the pit and rescue him. An elbow caught Bennie in the eye, and he was pushed back out again, squeezing his eye shut, trying to keep track of Joey. The other Wizard was holding a skinny kid from behind, restraining him and yanking him out of the crowd.

"Fuck, that is just like Larry. He's actually trying to do the job. You're a dentist, Larry! Not a bouncer. Oh nooooooo..."

The kid had managed to twist himself around in Larry's arms and had pulled at Larry's jacket, trying to get away from him. Instead he had pulled out Larry's wand, startling them both. Larry lunged at the young man, picking him up neatly in one hand and ripping the wand away from him with the other before tossing him toward the waiting arms of the mosh pit.

"Don't do it, Larry. Please don't do it!"

It was too late. Larry's adrenaline was running high and his wand was in his hand, even as more slouching twenty-somethings were reaching out to pull him into the crowd. He swirled his wand, yelling something no one could hear as a pulse of energy pushed out from him, forcing the crowd into the shape of a C. Many of them rolled over on top of each other like human bowling pins. The Potty Mouths kept playing through the entire thing, seeming not to notice anything out of the ordinary.

Larry raised his wand again, pointing it toward the middle where he could see the glow of an exit sign in the distance. But before he could say anything or even twitch the wand, the Fixer was at his elbow, pulling him back.

Correk had gotten the emergency call sitting in his kitchen sipping a beer, recounting the entire day with Harkin for Leira. Suddenly, he was in Cleveland stopping the Sons of Wizardry from harming a slew of punk rock fans. Larry looked at Correk, wild eyed but lowered his wand. "Get me outta here," he yelled, the other Wizards piling up behind him.

The Fixer turned toward the mosh pit, letting a thin stream of magic curl unseen into it till it found the one missing Wizard. Joey was still intact, but his hair was wild, and he was swiping and punching at anyone nearby trying to get out. The energy wrapped around the Wizard and acted as a repellent to everyone else. They pulled back leaving just enough room for Joey to finally slip out, weaving and bobbing his way toward Bennie. "I think they loosened a tooth."

Larry's spell wore off, unleashing the crowd again as they bent back toward the Wizards. "Time to go," said Correk in a sound tunnel, the words easily reaching all twelve of the Wizards as he circled his finger over his head.

Correk pushed the men in the direction of the door they had entered. He got to the door, making his way by them and let his eyes glow with his back to the crowd, easily unlocking the door and escorting the men to the relative safety of the hallway.

"Hey, what are you doing out here?" yelled the manager. "I'm not paying you if you don't do the work." Correk ignored his continued cries and led the men toward the side door and finally, back out to the alley. The dozen men immediately started talking at once.

"We're supposed to be at an Abba concert."

"My wife is gonna kill me."

"I think my tooth really is loose."

"This is not the guys trip I had in mind."

"What about Abba?"

Correk waved his arm over their heads, sucking the volume out of the air and waited patiently till they caught on and calmed down. "You," he said, pointing to Bennie. "What happened?" He snapped his fingers and Bennie's voice returned.

Bennie sucked in air and waved his hands in the air. "We're supposed to be at an Abba concert. We have great tickets! But somehow the asshole at the hotel got us here and they took one look at us and thought we were the muscle to keep those goons in check. We need to be at the concert. For some of these guys it took months of savings to get here."

Correk bit his lip to hide a smile. "Easily fixed," he said, growing a ball of light in his hand. He let the ball grow, pulling it apart to open a portal in the dark alley. On the other side was a similar alley but this time to Jacobs Pavilion. The faint sounds of *I Have a Dream* could be heard.

"I love that song," said Larry, quickly making his way through the portal.

"If you hurry, you won't have missed much," said Correk, stepping through with them. He swirled his hand in a circle and twelve tickets appeared in his palm. "Sometimes I really like this job," he said, as he handed out the tickets.

"Thank you," said Bennie. "You really saved our whole trip."

"Don't mention it," said Correk, smiling broadly as he waved. The Sons of Wizardry wasted no time in hustling down the alley toward the front of the building, disappearing around the corner.

Correk watched them go even as he was already opening a portal back to his kitchen. But when he stepped through, he found a note leaning against his beer bottle and no sign of Leira.

"Bounty job came up. Be back as soon as possible," he read out loud. "Great," he said with a sigh, picking up his beer and taking a swig. "Maybe I can play some Abba for the troll while I wait. Yumfuck?" The sound echoed in the house and there was no answer. "Dance party of one, coming up," he said, tipping back his beer and wandering into the living room, singing, "Can you hear the drums Fernando."

CHAPTER EIGHTEEN

Leira crouched in a field in the middle of Gretna, Nebraska that overlooked a row of warehouses in the distance. Next to her was Doc Leahy kneeling in the tall grass. Behind them were miles of farmland that had already been harvested for the season.

"Sorry about the meeting place. This one couldn't wait." Doc sneezed into his elbow and pulled a handkerchief out of his jeans pocket, wiping his nose. "Damn allergies."

"I get it and I'm here now. Tell me the details that I need to know. Why did you want to meet near the problem?"

"Because even with all your abilities, this one is going to take both of us." He lifted a knee off the wet ground, rocking back on his boots. "What you're looking at there is a giant drug lab that caters to magicals."

Leira turned to look at Doc. "That's a thing? Why would a magical want a drug? I mean, wouldn't a spell do the trick?"

"Every living creature knows anxiety of some kind.

Magicals and humans are the only ones who can make a big deal out of it."

"I see your point. A dog doesn't sit at home worrying about where the kibble is going to come from next month."

"No spell can really get rid of lingering doubt or worry. That's more of an inside job."

"I don't think I can even imagine a magical strung out on something."

Light bled out of one of the warehouses in the middle and large trucks could be seen pulling up outside. Leira pulled in just enough energy to track them. "They're not all magicals. This just keeps getting more interesting."

"Money motivates everyone. There's a flower that's grown on Oriceran outside the Kingdom of Virgo. It's called a lillio and looks a lot like a peony on this planet with all its delicate petals. Except when the lillio petals are harvested and crushed into a liquid they become a concentrated hallucinogenic for most magicals. Just getting it on your skin can be enough."

"Is that why you told me to bring these gloves?" Leira held up heavy purple gloves normally used to handle artifacts.

"That's exactly why and in a high enough dosage that drug can kill you. There aren't enough Jasper Elves around to know what exactly the effects would be, but I don't want to take chances. Even in a diluted form, when it comes into contact with a Kilomea it is very dangerous. It tends to bring out their most aggressive traits and ramp them up tenfold."

"That would mean killing just for sport." Leira watched one of the large doors open and caught a glimpse of a large metal vat before the door was shut again.

"That's about the extent of it. On Oriceran the kingdoms have banned growing the lillio and anyone found with even petals will spend some time at Trevilsom."

Leira watched everyone going about their job. She took note that they were all going about their well-established routines. "This didn't spring up yesterday. That thing is running like a machine. Why the sudden urgency in the middle of the night?"

"One reason is because I finally nailed down the location of their biggest processing plant," said Doc Leahy, nodding toward the warehouse. "The other is because they're just about to unleash their first big shipment, which will change everything here on this planet between humans and magicals."

"Does this lillio have any effect on humans?"

"None at all that we can tell, but if a human has any magical blood, then it will. There are a lot of humans who don't know their entire ancestry. Plus, get enough strung out magicals, mix in Silver Griffin agents going to ground and suddenly magic is exposed but there's no one around to clean up the mess. Oh, and there's one more reason that I think will interest you. The company behind this very expensive undertaking is called Fleeker, based just outside of Austin, Texas."

"Son of a bitch. It's like you just said Beetlejuice three times, only worse. Wolfstan Humphrey... again. Now you have my full and undivided attention. How do we take this thing out without bringing on the wrath of an entire zombie army?"

"Very carefully and without much finesse. I'm thinking one big boom."

Leira gave him a crooked smile. "I like the way you're thinking. But I have an even better idea before we get started. Let's get a lay of the land. As a rule, I like to know who I'm blowing up."

"There's no way we can get any closer," said Doc, concern growing. "The wards are dead ahead and if we trip one of those the game is over..."

Leira held up a hand, cutting him off. "There are more kinds of magic in this world than we have yet to discover. Don't move a muscle." Leira ducked down into the tall grass and let the energy flow through her, the symbols lighting up her arms.

"Now the bounty hunter is a philosopher," muttered Doc Leahy.

Leira set an intention, *go look,* and released the magic, flowing out ahead of her. At the last moment she gripped Doc's shoulder, connecting their magic. She looked at him with glowing eyes, smiling.

"How is this possible?" His mouth hung open as he turned to look at the large warehouse, images passing through his head.

"Jasper Elves with the spark of humanity. We're the bodiddily. A word I picked up from an old friend named Estelle." Leira felt the tug in the middle of her belly. Her eyes scanned back and forth as the magic slid easily through the wards, passing through the walls of the warehouse. Lined up down the left and the right were tall metal towers with ladders hanging off the sides. Down the center, tables were set up with cardboard boxes. Rolls of bubble wrap sat nearby on tall dispensers. Every time a box was filled and taped shut it was passed off to another worker who carried it to a pile that was growing taller and wider.

On the side of each box was the Fleeker logo. Leira felt the creep of anger inside of her and the magic hesitated, turning back to ask her if the intention had changed. The symbols on her arms started flipping in a different direction, predicting more outcomes.

She took in a deep breath, feeling Doc's apprehension grow, interfering with her concentration. *Hold the breath, keep it steady.* The stream of energy wove in and out of blue metal barrels brushing up against a Wood Elf in white coveralls that covered his feet and ended in a large helmet with an air supply. He cocked his head slightly, hesitating and looking down at the samples he was carrying. Worry passed across his countenance, but he shook it off and kept moving. *Magic can pass through one of those things. Good to know.*

Almost everyone in the warehouse was wearing protective gear from head to toe. But there were also people dotted here and there dressed in blue coveralls with gloves and masks as the only protection. *They've figured out who's one hundred percent human and who's not.*

Leira took note of how many bodies were inside the building and the position of the vats and processing before letting the magic recede and pull back through the wards, across the ground to her. She suddenly sucked in air and let go of Doc's shoulder. He rolled onto his back and was looking up at the stars, his hands pressed against the ground. "What a fucking ride! How did you do that?"

"I don't really see it as me doing it as much as getting out of the way. It never feels like the energy belongs to me. More like it's agreed to come out and play with me." She nudged Doc with her shoe. "We have a bigger problem if this mission is going to get anywhere."

Doc pushed himself up on his elbows, his long hair hanging down his wet back. He blinked his eyes a few times and shook his head. "I'm beginning to see the appeal of lillio. Irony grabs you by the short hairs at the oddest moments."

"Focus Doc. There's an entire warehouse that's already processed. Blowing it up will only put that stuff into the air or the water or both. We could end up interrupting their operation but helping Wolfstan with his end goal. We create the chaos. How do you get rid of dangerous magical waste?"

Doc sat all the way up. "Two ways. Alter it into something else or remove it to where no one ever sees it again."

"The first one is preferred," said Leira. "Do you know how to change it into something else? Neutralize it?"

"No, or I'd have mentioned that first. Lillio has always been resistant. It absorbs what it's mixed with, and if anything, becomes stronger."

"Then we have to move it, which takes logistics and time." Leira shook her head. "Wolfstan keeps finding some small twist that complicates everything. There has to be a third option and I have an idea but it's going to take some outside help from the old Fixer."

Doc Leahy suddenly stood up straight, announcing their presence in the field. Leira pulled him down, resting a knee on his chest as he struggled to get back up. "I'm freakishly strong even without the magic," she said. "Quit struggling like a beetle on its back and take a breath."

"You don't understand. The Fixer and I have history. Remember who I used to be?" He raised his eyebrows, scowling.

Leira let up and removed her knee as Doc sat back up, holding up his hands. "I'm calm. I won't stand up again. You caught me off guard. You move so fast, I wasn't sure if you somehow already called him with that magic of yours."

"What kind of history?"

"The very bad kind. I helped out particular Wizards and Witches that he would have preferred to see finally die. He came after me a few times to interrupt the pipeline, but the families were always one step ahead of him. Let's just say, these days we have a kind of understanding. If he doesn't see me, we let the past lie."

"You had to know if you got involved with me your paths would cross."

"The thought occurred to me, but I was trying to be careful."

"That's a good thought with Wolfstan Humphrey but it never works out. Defeating him is like the worst game of whack-a-mole and takes a group effort. We need to call Turner." Leira tilted her head to the side, still crouched. "You should do it. Don't hide from him, he'll respect you more."

Doc Leahy didn't say anything, working his jaw and glancing back at the warehouse and then at Leira.

"You've changed, Doc and we all deserve a second or third or however many chances it takes. I get the idea you've done some things that weigh on your shoulders.

Don't let this be one of them and especially not right now." Leira pulled out her phone and found Turner's phone number. She held out the phone to Doc. "Call him, and fast. Those boxes looked ready to ship and Wolfstan is back on his heels. He wants a win badly."

Doc reluctantly took the phone from her and held it back toward her face. "You need to unlock it," he said, with a grimace. He took it back and pushed the green button. "This will not have the happy ending you're looking for..."

"I find it better not to write the endings and work with whatever's in front of me instead."

Doc's eyes widened as someone picked up.

Hello Doc. Took you long enough. Only, what, a hundred years or so?

Doc was about to answer but he felt Turner's hand on his shoulder in the dark before he saw him.

"You are seamless with that abracadabra appearing stuff," said Leira.

"You knew this would happen!" Doc was breathing rapidly, his chest visibly moving up and down.

"He's not going to eat you. Turner, tell him you won't turn him to a puff of smoke." Turner carefully unfolded a small chair and took a seat in the tall grass but didn't answer. Leira shook her head and pointed at the warehouse. "Funny on any other day, Turner. Take a page from everything you've taught me and move it along."

Turner pursed his lips but relented. "The scales are not balanced in your favor. You've done things that should have sent you to Trevilsom till the end of time." Turner paused, leaning closer to Doc who was doing his best not to move or turn away. "It's fortunate for you that sometimes we get the chance to create good in this world that chips away at all the rest. It's clear that you've been doing that for generations. We aren't finished with this, but as long as you stay on the path you've chosen, I will work with you."

Doc put out his hand. "I'm sorry. There are too many things for me to list, but I remember every one of them and I regret them all. I'm sorry."

Turner took his hand and shook it. "Let the rest of your life be your amends and we will be square."

"I'll take that as a win for both of you." Leira rested a knee on the ground. "Now, if we could get back to the kerfuffle in the warehouse. Turner, there's a shit ton of lillio juice in that building that's been processed into what looks like small vials. Most of it is already boxed and ready to go. And the boxes all have that keen Fleeker logo on the sides."

"You need my help to dispose of it."

"Kind of. Until someone figures out how to neutralize it, we need your help to put it somewhere that's not really anywhere and lock the door on it. Like all the fun rooms in your house. But here's the kicker."

"So just creating space where there wasn't any on a different plane wasn't enough for you? And I thought we talked about not telling anyone."

"I haven't said enough to mean much of anything," said Leira, shaking her head.

"Different plane?" Doc Leahy held up his hand. "What kind of magic do you two possess?"

"None of your business," said Turner, letting out a sigh. "Fine, Leira, tell me the kicker."

"We need to move it all now and as a unit without the permission of all those goons inside. Oh, and without spilling a single drop of it or actually touching it ourselves." She wrinkled her forehead and stopped talking. *Hagan's rule number one, sort of. Let him process it.*

"It can't be done. I'm sorry. Those are too many factors. But there may be an alternative. We can trap the workers in another dimension. Drive them in there and shut that door, temporarily. That gives us time to move everything else. Not much time, knowing Wolfstan, but enough."

"How long does it take to create one of those planes of existence."

"Moments. Those rooms don't obey all of our rules, clearly."

"Then all we have left is the part about driving them into the trap. Finally, we kick some ass," said Leira brushing off her hands.

"Sounds easy," said Doc with an edge to his voice.

"Not your best pep talk, but it'll have to do. We have a warehouse to empty," said Leira, standing up.

"What are you doing? I thought that was off the list," snarled Doc Leahy.

Turner Underwood smiled and stood up next to her. "She's trying the direct approach. Badass. I like it."

"Turner you swear you can open up a large enough door to this new place in a flash?" Leira waved her arms over her head. "Hey, over here!"

"Have I ever given you a moment of doubt about anything?"

"You know, you never have. Let's not start today."

Doc Leahy let out a sigh and shrugged, slowly rising to

his feet and taking his place next to the other two. "Fine. We roll together. Do we have an actual plan?"

"Yeah, get out of there alive without scrambling our magic or our brains." Leira waved her arms again, the magic surging up her spine. "Hey jackasses! Over here!" Leira put two fingers in her mouth and let out a sharp whistle.

"Old school. Nice." Turner made sure his bowler was tight on his head and folded up his chair, continuing to fold it till it was small enough to fit in his pocket. He snapped his fingers as a cane slid out of his hand, ending in a round silver top without adornment.

"Why hasn't your side taken over completely?" asked Doc in astonishment.

"Don't get too dazzled by the small things. Our side, which includes you, Doc, has lines we won't cross. That always leaves a slight crack in the odds for the others to step into. That's the real secret Wolfstan Humphrey has discovered. Normalize cruelty and cheating and mix it with power. Legitimate power works the best. Stir in as much chaos as possible and before you know it, old norms are gone, and everyone is off kilter. Okay, we've been spotted." Turner waved at the workers in hazmat suits running out of a slim opening in the large door at the front of the warehouse. They were peering into the darkness and shouting to each other, scrambling back into the building and back again with more recruits.

"Looks like they have a small army," said Doc.

"At least they all look like volunteers who still have all their parts." Leira opened her hand and a large fireball appeared. "This will need an assist, Turner, to get through the wards. You are a known genius at that," said Leira, glancing at him.

Turner chortled and raised his cane, pointing it toward the warehouse. "Spatium satis iustum," he roared. "Now!"

Leira reared back, lifting her front leg and pitched the flames at the largest cluster of workers gathered toward the front. The fireball passed through the wards, slicing into several smaller fiery balls seeking out their targets.

"Nice touch," said Leira. "I did not see that coming. That was even a little artful."

Turner doffed his hat and took a slight bow. Doc Leahy rolled his eyes and pulled out his wand. "I suppose I will need the same kind of help."

"That spell is still hanging in the air, Wizard. I'm the old Fixer. My spells have staying power."

Leira pitched another fireball, watching it split again and divide into three different directions as workers ran and ducked behind larger objects. "Could you two stop talking about your wand sizes and help me provoke these people?"

Doc Leahy leaned back, circling his wand over his head and whipped it forward, unleashing a spray of pepper balls. The workers scattered, some of them running into the warehouse to hide.

"We want to get them angry, not run away entirely," said Turner, irritated. "Tone it down."

"Sorry..." muttered Doc Leahy. "This is my first time trying to get the psychopaths to run after me."

"Wait a second." Leira pointed toward the warehouse. "Doc, you may have the golden touch. Seems a little pepper on the skin is just enough to really piss you off. They're opening the gates. Wow, this is working out so far." She gave a crooked smile. "Kind of makes you nervous for the rest, huh Doc?"

"Not funny," he said, watching the doors open and hundreds of workers pour out, running toward them.

"Does that look like it's just about everybody?" asked Leira.

"I'd say, give one or two," said Turner Underwood.

"Perfect." Leira threw two more fireballs, watching them sail over the workers heads and turn back. It didn't take long for the surging crowd to notice and start to run faster toward Leira.

"They're getting closer," said Doc, swiveling his head back and forth between the dark, open field behind them and the angry mob running toward them.

"Keep lobbing something but let's back up a little," said Turner. "Don't want to be too obvious."

"Or die," said Doc as he backed up, throwing a volley of sparks with sharp points on the ends.

"I'm pretty sure I can't outrun them all." Doc moved a little further away as the first few came within a hundred yards of them.

"Now, Turner! Open the door!" Leira held her ground, throwing with a little more accuracy as Turner raised his arms over his head and whispered an ancient spell, his cane clutched in his right hand. Just in front of them a shimmer went across the air, stretching out several yards to either side. Leira watched in awe as the workers pushed toward the room, abruptly disappearing from the field.

Leira set an intention, pulling up more magic and set

the grass behind the remaining few on fire, distracting them from the trap.

"That's the last one," said Turner, lowering his arms. "We don't have a lot of time. A room built that quickly is unstable." He shrugged. "I didn't want to mention it before. I thought it might make you nervous. Especially you," he said to Doc. "We've only got a few hours and then I have to let them all out or risk leaving them stranded in a place worse than the world in between."

"Why don't you do that?" asked Doc, waving his arms around in the space where the rushing bodies had once been.

"See? This is what I mean. I thought I explained it," said Turner, tapping his cane hard on the wet ground. "We don't cross certain lines. Mass execution is one of them. Let's get some help. We have about two hours, maximum and then they can have their empty warehouse back and explain it to Wolfstan themselves. That may prove to be a worse punishment than Trevilsom." Turner pulled out his phone and dialed. "Hello my dear. I have a rather large and delicate clean up job for you. It's immediate and has to be over quickly. Use my position for location. Thanks." He hung up and put away his phone letting out a satisfied sigh.

A small bubble of laughter escaped Leira. "First you dazzle with the most amazing magic and then you go gangster on me and use your phone to call a cleanup crew."

Portals started opening around them and magicals stepped through, all of them in clothes that belonged in the past. Leira smiled. "You called Winland to round up everyone in that magic city of yours. Very smart. They'll need to cover up first," said Leira, trudging across the field toward the warehouse. "Hey, does this mean if we move all of this junk to an unstable alternate realm, it could get lost there forever?"

"In theory, or it could turn back up at an inopportune place or do something else we haven't thought of... But in theory, yes." Turner laughed and strode behind Leira. "I have a place already constructed for moments like this. It's all good. Are you coming Doc? We'll need everyone."

"What a weird night," said Doc, "and I have seen some weird nights." He ran to catch up as more helpers kept arriving. "Maybe we can push the needle toward the light."

"That's the idea every single day," said Turner, tapping his hat and disappearing in a cloud of grey smoke, reappearing inside the warehouse near the first tall stack.

Leira put out her arm to stop Doc. "Slow your roll. Remember what he said about not getting caught up in the dazzle. You and I still need to put on the protective gear." She stopped Doc from wandering toward the pile of gear near the door. "I'm glad you found some amount of peace with Turner. You've earned at least that."

"Maybe, but I still have a long way to go. Someday maybe I'll tell you a few stories, but probably not."

"Fair enough, let's get this done. Clock's ticking."

Leira waited until the last of the shipments were gone and the refugees from old New York were headed home. She wearily opened a portal to the warm kitchen and smiled at the sight of Correk sitting at the table, his head down and softly snoring. She stepped through and looked back in time to see Wolfstan's workers stumble out of the room where they had been locked, still angry and looking around. Turner tapped his cane on the ground and was gone in a blink. It didn't take long for them to look toward the open warehouse and realize something was missing. Leira let the portal close, watching some run toward the warehouse and others scatter into the night. "They must already have met Wolfstan," she whispered as she went around the table and gently kissed Correk on his neck. He stirred in his sleep and raised his head, his eyes half open. "You're home," he said, smiling, holding out his arms to pull in Leira.

She gave into his hug and held his head against her belly. "Let's go upstairs and go to bed for what's left of this night."

"Interesting mission?" asked Correk, yawning as he rose.

"Yeah, in more than one way. I'll tell you everything tomorrow over breakfast tacos. Come on," she said, taking Correk's hand and leading him toward the stairs. She paused at the sound of the troll laughing, her brow furrowing. "Did you hear that? I could have sworn I heard more than one troll."

"No, Nibbler isn't supposed to be here till tomorrow with your dad. You're just tired," said Correk, following her up the stairs. "I smell bayberry. Did Turner show up?"

"I can get very little past you. He came to help," she said, passing across the landing to the next flight of stairs. She looked toward the troll's room and saw a light move under the door but didn't hear anything. "Too tired to care," she muttered.

"Do you get some things past me?" asked Correk as they climbed the last few stairs and made their way into their bedroom. Leira shut the door behind them and slipped out of her shoes and her jeans, pulling her shirt over her head. "We can talk about that later too."

Correk grinned sleepily and pulled off his boots, sliding out of his jeans and t-shirt. Leira pulled back the covers and pulled him closer to her. "All that matters is right here and now."

CHAPTER NINETEEN

Jackson sat on the stairs of the Lincoln Memorial, occasionally looking back at the two trolls jumping from one giant stone knee to the other on Lincoln's statue. "I still don't see why Leira thought this would be good for us," muttered Jackson. "That girl definitely has me wrapped around her finger," he added, grinning.

He looked back again and realized the trolls were nowhere to be seen. He stood up and scanned the large statue but there was no glimpse of wild green or purple hair. "Uh oh. I thought I said to stay nearby." Jackson tapped the side of his head. "Think like a troll. Where would I go if I were a small troll? Some place with food..."

Jackson looked up and realized people were walking past him at a clip, holding up their phones in the direction of the reflecting pool. "Maybe that's a coincidence." He came down the stairs and started following everyone else, picking up his pace the closer he got to the water. Tourists were gathered around the nearest end, smiling and pointing their phones in one direction. "No, nope, nah ah.

Leira will have my head." He jogged the rest of the way, pushing his way to the front of the press of people and saw Yumfuck and Nibbler in the water, diving for quarters. Each time one of them got a quarter they would swim to the side and place it in the pile before paddling back out again."

"Did you see the trained rats?" asked a grey haired man, pointing them out for Jackson.

"Yeah, what a marvel," said Jackson, trying to catch Yumfuck's eye without calling his name. Yumfuck finally saw him and waved, spouting water out his mouth like a fountain. He lay on his back in the water and floated, paddling backwards in a circle to the cheers from the crowd. Nibble deposited another quarter to the side of the pool and joined Yumfuck doing a decent imitation of a doggie paddle. Jackson did his best angry face to no effect. Instead, the trolls pointed and laughed as others started to look at Jackson and back at the trolls.

"Are those your pet rats?" asked a woman, lifting her phone toward Jackson's face.

"Never was, never will be," said Jackson, hurriedly, his eyes glowing as he set an intention to let the Jasper magic spread across the reflecting pool. People froze right where they were, cameras raised, heads together pointing. Magicals in the crowd looked up surprised and over at Jackson, hurrying away to another tourist attraction.

Jackson jumped into the reflecting pool and bobbed his way quickly toward the two trolls, scooping them up and pushing back through the water to the side.

"What about our quarters?" yelled Nibbler. "We worked hard for those."

"They're not yours, first of all. They're wishes and belong in the water. Second, you don't need them, and we have just five minutes to get the hell out of the vicinity."

"We need foooooood," pleaded Yumfuck. "Those quarters were going to buy us lots of food."

Jackson hoisted himself out of the reflecting pool and stuffed the trolls, one in each pocket as he ran from the scene in the direction of the Washington Monument. Yumfuck landed in the pocket with his butt sticking out and it took him a minute to turn topside and poke his head out. He waved to Nibbler. "Aloha motherfucker!" he said cheerily. "Where are we headed?"

"Anywhere fast," huffed Jackson, making good time toward the obelisk in the distance. He heard the chatter pick back up behind him and glanced backward to see everyone starting to move about again. Most of them were scratching their heads and trying to remember what they had just been doing. He breathed a sigh of relief and kept moving, not wanting to remind anyone of the two rambunctious trolls.

They came to the benches close to the monument and Jackson landed heavily, still breathing hard from his run and sense of panic across the short, grassy distance. Yumfuck leaned out of the pocket, almost tipping over to get a better look at Nibbler. "Hey, I'll bet you I can get more rides from people up to the top of the Washington Monument."

Nibbler started to shake his head and put out his tiny paw to shake.

"Oh no you don't. You two aren't going anywhere. Leira specifically said no more camera time for you, Yumfuck."

"Don't worry. No one will ever know we're hitching a ride on them. We'll even keep it moving so they don't accidentally spot us."

"Yeah!" Nibbler chimed in.

"Sure, nothing could go wrong with that. No can do. I'll walk you up to the top myself but only if you stay hidden in my pockets. Deal?"

"Hey, what's wrong with that guy?" Yumfuck pointed to a man with dark hair except for a striking streak of silver. He was pushing his way through the crowds just outside the monument, looking in every direction. "There's a wand sticking out of his pocket."

"Yumfuck, that's rude," said Jackson. "And you don't need euphemisms. We use the real words for body parts."

"Hey, are those guys after him?" Nibbler scrambled out of Jackson's pocket and onto the bench, running to the edge and leaning against the metal frame.

Jackson slowly rose, a chill going down his spine and a hum along the back of his neck. "That's a Silver Griffin agent. Fuck me, that's Ernie." Jackson scanned the two grunts following Ernie and realized they were Kilomeas in a glamour. "Things do not look good for Ernie. His bad luck has returned. Kilomeas on a hunt, Yumfuck and Nibbler, and a city full of people watching us. How do we get him out of here?"

"We've got this," said Yumfuck, scrambling out of the pocket. "I am Batfuck," he shouted, leaping off the edge of the bench. "Come on, Robin."

"I told you, I'm SpiderTroll," said Nibbler, jumping after him.

"You know the fake out we made up when you slept over?" asked Yumfuck as they scurried toward Ernie.

"Yeah, five fun ways to fake out a human. Which one did you have in mind?" Nibbler ran around a trash can breathing in deeply and smiling even as he kept running.

"Number two and that lady right over there." Yumfuck pointed at an older woman with helmet hair, sprayed till it didn't move in the wind. She was wearing a pale Chanel suit and dangling from her arm, a matching leather purse. Nibble took his position on the sidewalk in front of the woman and stuck out his tongue, followed by a roar. The woman startled, screaming and pressing her hand to her throat.

Yumfuck ran toward a light pole and bounced off, landing neatly on the top of her purse and opening it in one swift motion. He had her wallet out before it had registered for her that a troll was hanging off her arm. "Hi ya, sister," said the troll with a salute, jumping down to the ground and running away with Nibbler by his side.

"My wallet! That gerbil stole my wallet!"

The two trolls ran straight past Ernie, who saw them and slowed down for a moment. "Yumfuck?"

They headed just to the left of the Kilomeas, tossing up the wallet as they passed by. The closest Kilomea, disguised as a construction worker in jeans and work boots with a plaid shirt on, caught the wallet, turning it over to get a better look at it.

"He stole my wallet! Thief! Thief!" yelled the woman, pointing at the Kilomea. The pair stopped, looking around at the people gathering closer with frightened and angry faces. A metro park police officer blew a large metal whistle and came running toward them, his partner in tow.

The trolls circled back, nimbly running between boots and sneakers and high heels till they reached Ernie who was closing in on the heavy traffic and Fourteenth Street. Jackson got to him first, slinging his arm around him and pulling him close. "I'm a friend and I can help you. I think you know my daughter, Leira Berens."

Ernie looked at Jackson, a sheen of sweat across his face despite the cool air. "Leira has a father?" he asked, startled, still trying to step into the street.

Jackson rolled his eyes and held him back. "Why is that so surprising to everyone? I didn't know. Never mind. We need to get you out of here and someplace safe."

"Starbucks is out. The trains are crawling with thugs looking for agents. They've got pictures of some of us and apparently, I'm one of them. Those two have been tracking me for a few miles since I left the train."

"Ernie, you're going to have to overlook this bit of magic out in the open, just this once..."

"What about that spell back at the giant pool?" asked Nibbler.

"Ernie, you're going to have to overlook a lot," said Jackson, scowling at Nibbler. "You're on my side, remember? Bonded? Jump on you two. This is gonna be quick and dirty, and hopefully successful."

Jackson put Ernie's shaking hand on his shoulder and pulled in magic, his eyes glowing and symbols appearing at the edge of his sleeves. He ignored the looks of the drivers whizzing by and threw shadows around the small group. Working fast, he opened a portal deep in the shadows to the inside of the Carousel Lounge. Uncle Petie came roaring out the back at the sound of a portal opening, ready to defend this establishment or take in another refugee.

His brow furrowed when he saw Jackson and Ernie, but he didn't stop them. "Jackson, it's been a month of Sundays since you were here. I think your daughter was still living here. How is she?"

"She's good as far as I know. Moved out of town," said Jackson, pushing Ernie through the portal and stepping through, closing it behind himself before the shadows could dissipate. "Different kind of refugee for you, Uncle Petie. A Silver Griffin agent named Ernie. Think you could look after him for a while till we figure out what to do with him?"

"We always have room for one more. Besides, I still owe you from that last poker game."

"You still do, Uncle Petie. Ernie, you're in good hands. I have to get back to my daughter's place," he said, opening another portal to the hallway inside the townhouse.

"Thank you, I mean it," said Ernie. "I've been on the run for days. I don't know how much longer I would have lasted out there. They kept finding me."

"I'm glad you made it," said Jackson, grimly as he stepped through to the squeaky wooden floor. "Till we meet again but under better circumstances. Fight on," he said as the portal closed. "What is happening?" muttered Jackson, sparks skittering across the floor.

CHAPTER TWENTY

Leira sat at Marcy's kitchen table with the rest of the elderly residents sitting and standing around her. "We have a proposition for you," she said, glancing at Correk who was leaning against the refrigerator across the kitchen. "We need some help. Wolfstan has managed to create a maelstrom of trouble and we're spread too thin. There's just too many magicals to help or fires to put out."

"Whatever it is, we're in," said Portia, hurriedly, pounding her fist into her palm. "It's about time we joined the fight."

"Yeah," said Elijah. "It's been frustrating watching from the sidelines. Yumfuck has been keeping us up to date."

"Yeah, I think he sees all of you as a part of his family. He doesn't do that as easily as everyone thinks he does. That's how I know we can trust you. Plus, I heard Portia and George are retired agents? That's perfect. You'd be off the Silver Griffins roles so no one is hunting you, but you still have your skills."

"Ready to serve," said George, standing up straighter.

"Here's a short list of a few magicals in this area. It's just three and all Light Elves. We have some intel that leads us to believe one of them may be targeted by Wolfstan Humphrey for his experiments. There seems to be a pattern with who he chooses. Like there's a DNA component or a biological factor that plays a part."

Correk crossed his arms. "Wolfstan may not have as much information as we do about rearranging cells, but that doesn't mean he hasn't figured out some unique things we didn't even think of."

Marcy took the piece of paper and ran her finger down the list. "If we see anything suspicious, what do you want us to do?"

"First," said Leira, holding up her hands, "keep your distance. I don't want to see something horrible happen to anyone here. Do not engage." She looked each of them in the eye, arching a brow. Portia bit the inside of her cheek trying to hide a smile.

"Look at that. The youngest one here is trying to give us the stink eye." George couldn't hide his amusement.

"I know," said Leira. "You've all probably faced some decent sized monsters in your long lives. But this is different. I've only known one other who was like Wolfstan and that was Rhazdon."

Emmett sucked in a bit of air, growing pale. "We are very familiar with Rhazdon. She hurt so many people."

"Wolfstan is on track to do the same and in two worlds. Don't underestimate him. Don't take on a fight just because you think you might win. Call in the location immediately and we'll drop everything and come running. We want to capture some of Wolfstan's goons associated with this project and interrogate them."

"Can we help with that too?" asked Portia, her face growing redder with anger. "I have a few ideas."

"As much fun as that would be, we're after information, not revenge." Leira got up from the table. She handed Portia a piece of paper. "Learn this spell. If you see anything, use it. That will get straight to me and Correk and will be like a magical 911 call. We'll know to come right away."

"Ollie, ollie... We've known this spell since we were small," said Portia.

"Read the ending. It has a twist, courtesy of the Fixer."

"Use the spell and bend your fingers just like this," said Correk. "You'll need to be precise."

They all practiced, encouraging each other until each one could do it without fumbling any of the parts.

"Keep practicing so you can do it when faced with a monster and your heart is pounding." Leira hugged Portia and then Marcy, working her way through the group till she got to Correk and took his hand. They walked to the kitchen door to go out the back way. "I have your word? No interventions?"

"Cross our hearts," said Emmett, making an X over his heart.

"We'll do our best," said Marcy, making Leira pause at the threshold and look back.

"Sounds like something you'd say," muttered Correk, "without the swearing."

"You love my swearing," said Leira as she kept going out the door.

"I love everything about you."

The door shut and Portia put her arm across George's back. "That was us a few hundred years ago. Clothes have gotten better. So has the love."

CHAPTER TWENTY-ONE

L ouie took his mug out of the microwave and took a sip. *Still cold.* He spit it back into the cup and looked behind the machine. It was plugged in. "Come on. Broken?" He scratched his head and looked at his wand laying on the counter. "Just one spell. Who's gonna come and get me these days, anyway?" He scooped it up and tapped the edge of his mug, watching the liquid gurgle, and steam rise out of the cup. He put the wand down and picked up the mug, slurping out of the top. "Perfection."

"I... uh... I'm sorry." Ava Hou's voice echoed in the quiet apartment.

Louie spit out his coffee, choking on what was in his mouth, coughing and spitting as he hastily put the cup down. Coffee splashed over the sides, burning his hand as he turned, trying to slide the wand behind him on the counter. "I didn't hear you come in. How... how long have you been standing there? I mean, what can I do for you? How's your day?" He bit his bottom lip, choking on the remaining questions that wanted to jump out of his mouth.

Ava had one arm tucked behind her, and she was blinking, pressing her lips together. She was dressed in her usual uniform of jeans and a colorful shirt with matching Keds. A tear rolled down her cheek and she quickly brushed it away, setting her jaw.

"Oh, hey..." Suddenly, Louie forgot about what he'd been doing and rushed to her, holding on to her arms. "Are you okay? Has something happened?" He hugged her to him, breathing in the smell of roses coming from the top of her head. He let go and held her out again. "Say something."

"You know how much I care about you," she said haltingly, her eyes shining.

"Oh no, this is the beginning of the breakup conversation. I know those words. I've used those words." He let go of Ava and clamped his hands down on the top of his head, spinning around and pacing the tiny living room. "Was it something I said? I mean, I've been told more than once by anyone who's met me that I can talk too much. Occasionally something spills out sideways. I didn't mean it, or I did mean it, whichever it is."

"Louie, you're gonna need to take a breath. I can't get a word in and you're already halfway down the wrong road."

"What?" Louie stopped moving and put his hands down. "You said, wrong road."

"I did, but the right one you may not like either." She put up a hand to stop him. "Why don't we give me the floor till I say I'm done?"

"I can work with that. Should I take a seat? I'll take a seat." He sat down on the old sofa, moving a little to get away from the one bad spring.

Ava ducked her chin, her dark hair falling like a thick

curtain around her face. She started speaking, still looking down at her blue Keds. "I know there is magic in the world."

"Um..." Louie started to speak but Ava clenched her hands into fists at her side and Louie knew better than to keep going.

"I know about Oriceran." She looked up at Louie whose eyes were wide. "I've known since I was a little girl. My father, Li Wei Hou is not just a businessman, he's a Keeper. Only one of ten honored Keepers in this world." Louie sat back against the couch and Ava finally moved from the spot by the entrance, shutting the door and coming to perch on the edge of the one chair. "Magicals from Oriceran often underestimate humans. We're seen as great inventors of engines or computer parts or blue tooth. But not magical. Not what you think of as special, even though there is something called the spark of humanity." She shook her head, tucking her hair behind her ear and folding her hands in her lap. "I know you've probably heard of it. Most magicals know something about it, but most also discount it. It's thought of like an appendix. Maybe it did something at one time, but not anymore. They're all wrong."

"I know about Leira and what it did when mixed with her Jasper blood, but that's rare."

"That's what I'm talking about." Her hands moved through the air as she spoke. "It's not rare, just hidden. It's ironic. All of magic is hidden from millions of human beings, and you accept that as a fact. Normal. But it never occurs to you that maybe there's more that is hidden from you, and with good reason. There was a time when the spark of humanity was revered, and everyone knew about it. It was the last time the gates were fully open thousands of years ago. But there's a dark side to magicals."

"I'm well aware."

"I mean far more magicals than you do. A mistrust of what is different and can't be controlled. Or in the case of those with the spark, who can see the real you."

"You lost me." Louie leaned forward, his arms resting on his knees. Ava watched him working at being patient and her expression softened.

"The spark doesn't only enhance magic. That's actually just a side benefit. It's real ability when found in a human being at full strength is that it gives the person the magic to see someone's true character. Their humanity. It's impossible to lie to someone who has the spark. They'll always know."

"I can see how that would get on some magicals' nerves."

"The persecution started as fights between neighbors who felt judged or who had lied. That grew into skirmishes and progressed to wars. Magicals and humans who were known to be in the family lines with the spark were targeted and went into hiding. It didn't take long before their numbers dwindled." Ava bit her bottom lip and stopped, staring out the window.

"Do you want some water? It's about all I have. Not very good at the domestic thing," said Louie, easily flipping over the back of the couch. In a few steps he was at the sink.

"Can you heat up more of that coffee?"

His face reddened and he seemed flustered, turning one way and then the other. "Sure, I suppose. Yeah, why not?"

He took a mug off the drying rack and poured coffee into it, picking up his wand with his other hand. "Man, why is this so awkward? Like we should have gone on a date first."

Ava rose and walked up behind Louie, putting her arms around him and resting her head on his back. "That's because magic in some ways is so intimate. I understand that."

Louie turned in her embrace and leaned down to kiss her. "You didn't really want that coffee, did you?"

"No, I do," she said, smiling, kissing him again and letting go to lean on the counter behind her.

"Consider it done." Louie tapped the edge of her mug as the coffee began to roil and steam. He handed it to Ava and stepped back staying quiet, still holding onto his wand.

She blew across the top, taking her time. "To have the spark at its full strength can be a very lonely existence. The bearer knows immediately who likes them and who doesn't. For most people, that's hidden and even changes. And to love someone with the spark is to know that it's as if your mind is being read at the most inopportune moments. Imagine trying to have a normal argument where you don't even know why you're mad, but the other person does. If they share it, it feels like an invasion, if they don't, it feels like a lie. You can't win."

"Ava, do you love me?"

Ava's face reddened and her eyes opened wider, the cup still close to her lips.

Louie tilted his head to one side. "I already know you do. I can feel it in here and without any kind of spark. Just some human and Wizard blood mixed together. I think I loved you from the first moment I saw you, but I can be a little thick. And I've never felt this way before. It took me a while to realize it wasn't allergies. There's a smile." He twirled his wand between his fingers, end over end. "You must have known how I felt. But I'm not so thick that I don't get what you're saying about a dark road. Being able to put the pieces together is what's made me a good scavenger and kept me alive. Your pops wouldn't be a Keeper if he didn't have the whole shebang. One hundred percent of the spark, which means you have it? Your mother must have also carried it. Frankly, I'm flattered." He sat back, still twirling the wand, blue and white light flashing out of it, hitting the ceiling. "Back in the disco days, this trick killed every time."

"You are very weird, Louie. Why are you flattered?" Ava wiped her face with her sleeve and let out a shudder of relief.

"Your entire family can see right through me and Mr. Hou still rented me an apartment. On top of that, he must have known how I felt about you and I'm still alive. He didn't run me out of town. There are a lot more magicals who find out I'm a scavenger and nothing else who don't want anything to do with me. Sometimes being able to see someone for who they really are is an advantage. Besides, I'm kind of transparent. It's too much work to hide. I'd rather be hanging with Ronnie or even better, wrestling with you," he said with a grin. "Don't tell Ronnie. It would hurt his feelings."

"You don't care that there are times when I know more about you, than you do? Or that you'd never be able to tell me even a slight lie? Like, I didn't lend Ronnie the money from our retirement fund, or I've only had two beers, or yes, that dress does look good on you."

"I'll probably try to pull those off anyway. I'm always looking for the angles, and once in a while I find one where no one was looking. No, you're gonna catch me slip sliding on occasion, but you'll love me anyway. I have a pretty good feeling about that."

"You're taking this all really well. It's like I found the one person who could roll with the real me."

Louie took the mug out of her hand and put it on the counter, wrapping his arms back around her. "That's some real magic," he said kissing her neck. His wand was still in his hand.

"Then I have something I have to show you. Louie, we can do this later," she said, playfully pushing him back.

"How about now *and* later?" he asked, trying to take her back in his arms.

"No, it has to be now in order for there to be a later."

"Wow, that was serious. It was like you got me to think about baseball in the middle of trying to kiss you."

"You're gonna thank me for that in about two minutes." She took his hand and lead him toward the door, opening it and pulling him out into the hallway.

"Where are we headed?" Louie shut the door behind them and shoved his wand quickly into his pocket as Ava pulled him down the hall toward the stairs.

"You'll see and just remember, it'll be okay," she said as they headed down the stairs.

"What does that mean?" Louie looked up, wondering if he should have brought his sword.

They wound down the stairs and out to the sidewalk to

a different door on the other side of the entrance to the restaurant. Behind the door were stairs leading down into a basement. Ava stopped halfway down and squeezed Louie's hand. "You trust me, right? I mean, I already know it, but you need to be really aware of it right now."

Louie searched her face, looking for clues. "Alright, I'm aware." His instincts were on high alert, just like when he was on Dead Man's Crawl or could smell a Kilomea nearby. Ava pulled him the rest of the way down the stairs and into the darkened room. He saw figures moving in the darkness and put his hand on his wand, ready for anything. Ava flicked on the light and in front of him was a ring of people, including Mr. Hou.

"We've been waiting for you. You took a little longer than we expected, but here you are." Mr. Hou stepped aside to show him two metal chairs with red vinyl seats. "This one is for you," he said pointing to the one on the left.

"I had to make a deal with the Society of the Keepers. In order to tell you about the spark of humanity and what it really is, and who we really are..." She stopped and licked her lips. "I had to agree for you that you'd be willing to be a part of our group. It was the only way that we could keep seeing each other," she said hurriedly. She leaned in closer. "Like you said, I knew that you loved me and yes, I love you too."

Louie cleared this throat and stepped up to the chair, sitting down. "Okay, what's involved in being a part of your group? Is it like a fraternity? Are there paddles or beer pong? As long as it's not like trying to join a Kilomea clan. Those boys are nasty with the..." He saw Ava doing micro shakes of her head, trying to signal him. "Sorry, I talk a lot when I'm nervous. Of course, you people probably already knew that. Or does it get that refined? Sorry, doing it again. It's part of my charm, some of the time. Ronnie likes it."

"Louie O'Donnell," said Mr. Hou. "That's the name you put on your lease. Is that your real name?"

"Yes, on my mother's side. She was a human from this world. Oriceran as a rule isn't big on last names. You belong to a kingdom and they're all your family."

Mr. Hou sat down next to him in the other chair and gestured to a man in a dark blue suit and red tie. The man brought over a large leather bound book and laid it in Mr. Hou's lap. Louie saw the cufflinks shoot out when the man handed over the book. *Lobbyist. Has to be.*

"He can be trusted," said Mr. Hou, looking deeply at Louie.

"You knew what I was thinking?"

"No, only how you felt about it. We see what people have come to believe about the world around them. It's a constant reminder that none of it is real. Change a belief, change the way you see the world."

Louie sat back and slid his wand into his pocket. He threw up his hands. "You're blowing my mind."

"That was expected. Magicals have a harder time believing in the human spark, than human beings do. Of course, not many over the years have been welcomed into our Society. Most would not be able to handle it, but Ava has made a convincing argument that you are unique."

"She means that as a compliment, I'm sure," said Louie, looking around at the somber faces. "Tough room."

"She explained to you our ability to detect someone's

true character? Did she include that we can affect the way a magical sees things by suggesting a different thought? You wouldn't even know it had happened."

Louie stopped talking and looked from Mr. Hou to Ava who was biting her bottom lip.

"I thought she might leave that part out. We don't have the ability to direct anyone's mind. You will always have free choice. But we can suggest options. It's a powerful and sometimes dangerous tool in the wrong hands."

"Do you ever intervene when a group of magicals are threatened?"

Mr. Hou grew worried and looked back at the others. "We are dedicated to peace and try to avoid conflict. Unfortunately, I guess, we can always see many sides to every argument."

"This is more about one monster named Wolfstan Humphrey who's turned a lot of innocent magicals against their wills into some kind of zombie army with spare parts. Could you reach someone like that and suggest another way?"

"It's possible," said an older, slender woman with long gray hair that gently framed her face wearing pale slacks and a bulky knit sweater. "We did something similar a thousand years ago to help a tribe being held captive so long they had forgotten how to fight. We reminded them."

"We're willing to serve when necessary," said someone else in the back of the group.

"I think I found a necessary."

"We will take a look at your request," said Mr. Hou. "But first, we need to complete our task here. Louie, you have a sword. A very special sword, I understand. It's legendary among our kind and can only be handled by the one it chooses. Am I correct?"

Louie looked at Ava who smiled weakly. "I saw you practicing with it."

"That's what I meant about you being unique. The sword chose you in part because you have the spark of humanity. Not as much as Ava, but it's there. The sword could sense it and your true nature. It bonded with you."

"Does this make us cousins?" Louie asked in a worried tone.

"No," said Mr. Hou, arching a brow. "You are not related to my daughter who I am sure you are treating with the utmost respect. This book," he said, tapping the cover, " is one of thousands. In them, we record everything we know about the spark of humanity and the people who carry it. Their stories are written down here. Somewhere in here are some of your ancestors. My family, the Hou's, have been part of this honorable service for centuries. Within these pages, you will learn about each of them. You will join us and become part of the protection that surrounds all of us."

"Not that I'm leaving or anything, but what exactly does that entail? I'm kind of already obligated to be helping out a certain Jasper Elf who would have way too many questions and hunt my ass down if I disappeared for too long. An occasional walkabout, sure."

"You will help keep the books hidden and when necessary, help out one of our kind. Ava will help you learn and train you further. Did you think there was no purpose for the Parkour?"

Louie clapped his hands together. "I'm ready, let's do this. Wait, does this mean Ava and I are together forever?"

Mr. Hou put his hand on Louie's shoulder. "One step at a time. First you take my daughter on a proper date and then we'll see what happens."

"All this just to date your daughter. That is intense."

"Do you agree to our terms? Once in the society, you cannot leave, so think hard."

"Guys," said Louie, holding out his arms. "You can sense my answer, right? If I say no, I lose Ava. Anything is worth staying with Ava. Besides, you seem fairly normal as spooky hidden groups with weird power go."

"Orange," said Ava in a hushed voice, getting glances from everyone in the room. Everyone but Louie who winked at her. In the middle of everything he heard her and understood.

"Yes, I'm in," he said with a smile and a nod. "Teach me."

CHAPTER TWENTY-TWO

Yumfuck came out onto the landing right outside his bedroom door and listened. "Leira?" he called out, but there was no answer. "Correk?" Still no answer. He put a paw to his ear but there were no sounds. He came and put his face between the spindles in the stair railings. "How do you put out a small house fire?" he yelled. No sudden sound of running feet or yelling.

No one was home. It was time to put the finishing touches on what he was building.

The troll slid down the banister, doing a loop off the end and landing neatly on his feet on the first floor. He ran to the basement door and pushed it open, scurrying down the stairs. Once he was there, he grew in size to four feet, switching on the light and looking at the last pile of lumber that was needed to finish the job. He easily hoisted the bundle tied with plastic around the middle onto his shoulder and climbed the stairs, turning off the light on his way.

He made his way through the house and up the stairs, careful not to hit the walls with the small pile of lumber. So far, over the weeks he had managed to avoid damaging anything on every trip. Sure, there were a few close calls in his room, but those he was able to repair.

"Too close to screw it up now," he said in a hushed voice.

He carried the wood into his room and set it down near his bed. By now that was the only open space still available except for a little real estate left around his dresser and his desk. He stepped back from his creation and took an inventory.

"Vending machine, check." One swift pull of a lever on the bright shiny metal machine and a bag of Doritos came sailing out, shooting over the four foot troll's head. "Still have to tweak that." He leaned over to his desk and added to his punch list. *Fix Doritos slot. Still shooting through the air.* The machine stood two feet high with coiled metal in four rows up and four rows across. In each coil were stacks of Oreos and Cheetos, Twizzlers and Reese's Cups, Pop Tarts and beef jerky. Almost all of Correk's stash.

"Next, obstacle course." The troll quickly shrunk down to five inches and approached the rope ladders stretched across the side of the machine. He clambered up to the top and walked across the netted walkways over the open space in the room, climbing near the ceiling. From there he grabbed onto the monkey bars, making his way over the bed, his feet dangling.

At last the troll made it to a tiny platform, three inches square where he grabbed onto a bar overhead and jumped, taking a zipline over near his closet all the way across the room. "Yeeeeehaaaaaaw," yelled the troll, who had not forgotten his Austin roots.

He landed neatly on the handle to the closet, his weight pushing down enough to open the door. Next, he jumped to a short and narrow bookcase in his room, doing a somersault off the top to the shelf below. He pushed on the side of the book, *Practical Magic*, tilting it to the right. The panel in the back of the bookcase slid over, revealing a small entrance fit for a five inch sized being. The troll walked through the secret door, his green hair grazing the top and he clapped his hands. A light came on illuminating the small bean bags from someone's game, tossed around the hang out room. A miniature cooler was tucked in a corner with a bottle opener hanging off the side. Tiny TV trays were folded along one wall that was painted a bright white. Perfect for a movie screen. In the ceiling of the secret room were built in speakers that were also placed around the room with a standard size sub-woofer on the floor near his bed.

The troll had already tested it out with a YouTube 4K video of surfers in Ventura Beach. He had felt the boom-boom in his chest from their music and the crash of the waves for hours after he turned it off. He had gone to sleep that night with a smile on his face.

"Siri, play Kidz Bop," he said as *Old Town Road* came blaring out of the speakers. The troll bopped his head in time with the music, dancing around the bean bags, diving underneath one and plopping down on another. He came up, breathing hard and grinning. All his tiny sharp teeth showing. "Next, my favorite part."

He came out of the secret room and pulled the book

back in place, the door sliding neatly across till it clicked. The troll rubbed his hands together and ran to one side of the bookcase and jumped up in the air, coming down on his back on a pale blue plastic slide. The structure made two sharp turns and a loop-di-loop, winding down through the closet and out the side where he had cut out a hole, big enough for trolls to fit through. He whizzed through, his hair flowing backward and his mouth open, his eyes wide with joy.

Directly behind the vending machine was a ball pit that could easily fit ten trolls and was filled with old ping pong balls. A trampoline was next to that with thick rubber bands instead of coils, laced along every side of a piece of stretch jeans fabric donated by Marcy from down the street.

All of the magical neighbors had contributed something to a complicated blanket fort built underneath his bed. The bed was normal size for an elementary school age kid, but underneath was perfect for a troll with at least a hundred years on him. Rimming the back of the blanket fort near three walls of the bedroom were tracks for regular sized dominoes that could be moved to form different curves and lines. When knocked over they sounded like marbles rolling across the floor.

He came out from the bed and stopped in the center of the room at the latest piece he had completed. A sand mandala in vibrant colors meant to bring health and happiness to all who played in his room. He let out a contented sigh, his paws on his hips as he looked over the landscape of the troll world he had built.

There was a soft tap at the door. "Yumfuck, you okay in there? Sounded like something came loose," said Leira through the door.

Yumfuck looked at the door and back at his masterpiece. "Maybe it's time," he muttered and went to open the door a crack. "How's your day going?" he asked, testing the waters before he opened the door any wider.

"Pretty good so far. Nothing's blown up, caught on fire or broken. Same for you?"

"Would you like to see?" He poked his head out the door, holding out his paw. "You need to be careful and you can only come in a few inches. That's it. I don't want anything to get wrecked. Deal?"

Leira crouched and took his paw. "Deal."

Yumfuck stepped back and pushed open his door, revealing what he had been working on in every spare moment for days on end.

Leira walked in just a few inches, watching the troll watching her. She sucked in air, marveling at each miniaturized structure designed for fun. "Yumfuck Tiberius Troll, you've outdone yourself. This is amazing. You even have speakers."

The troll beamed, putting his paws on his hips and poking out his furry chest.

Leira looked up toward the ceiling where *Call Me Maybe* was pouring out of a built-in speaker. "Is that surround sound? Did you do the electrical work?" She saw the shadow pass across Yumfuck's face and immediately regretted the question.

"You are even more amazing than I realized, Yumfuck.

A true craftsman. You've made an amusement park in your own room."

"There's a blanket fort. Portia collected the blankets for me," he said pointing under his bed. Leira got down on her hands and knees very carefully and peered underneath. "And there's a slide and a zip line and a ball pit... And more," he said, with his hand to the side of his mouth.

"What's the pile of lumber going to be?" asked Leira.

"Those will be shelves along this wall right here," he said, plastering himself against the wall near the door. "That's where all the potted plants will go. Troll cots for sleepovers. Once that's done, I'll have a place where my friends and my brothers and sisters can come and visit me."

Leira felt a pang in the center of her chest and her breath caught in her throat. "Oh," she said quietly, looking around at the room with a different view. "You made a place so you can have visitors and they'll feel welcomed." She curled her fingers into her hand to stop her eyes from welling up. "What a great idea. How long have you been thinking about this? I mean, this is pretty thorough. You must have drawn up plans for a while."

"Since the last Christmas in Austin when we had all the family together."

Leira quickly brushed a tear that had escaped off her cheek. "How many little ferns do you have over there?" she said, her voice cracking just a little in the middle.

"Fifty-two so far."

"Fifty two." The words came out slowly. "That's a lot of trolls. Yumfuck, when you lived on Oriceran, how many trolls did you usually sleep with?" She pressed her lips together, waiting for the reply.

"I don't know. At least a hundred," he said with a shrug.

Leira swallowed hard and bent down to scoop up the tiny furry troll. She held him against her cheek as he trilled. "Every troll in Oriceran will want to visit you, Yumfuck. When will the inaugural sleepover be happening?"

"As soon as Wolfstan Humphrey is no more. It'll be my way of celebrating and then I'll know, at least for a little while, you won't need my help. Should be good for a weekend, right?"

Leira blinked to hold back another tear. "You are a very fierce warrior and a loyal friend. That sounds like a great plan because one way or another we will defeat Wolfstan Humphrey, and soon." Leira took a closer look at the vending machine. "Hey, I don't suppose that's Correk's stash reissued."

The troll looked sheepish and shrugged, his claws crossed behind his back. "Maybe."

Leira set the troll down on top of his dresser. "I guess I've never said this to you before. If you need anything like this again, ask me. I'd be really excited about helping and pitching in. Maybe even add something?" The troll's smile dropped, and he looked around. "No?" asked Leira. "Okay, I get it. Your idea, your plans and your job to do. But if you ever need me, just like I need you, I hope you'll ask. This is a two-way street," she said, pointing to herself and then to the tiny troll. "We're not just bonded, we're family. Forever and then one more day."

The smile returned to the troll's face and he started pushing Leira toward the door. "Time to go. I have work to do. So do you. Hunt down Wolfstan Humphrey so we can get this party started."

Correk appeared at the door and immediately spotted the vending machine. "Are those my Pop-Tarts? And my Cheetos?" he asked, his voice rising.

"Not anymore," said Leira. "They've gone to a very good cause." She pushed gently on his chest, even as he gave some resistance. "But those were mine. Hey, did you use my hunting ropes for that walkway?"

Leira got Correk the rest of the way out of the room and turned back to give Yumfuck a wink, gently shutting the door. "We need to do better by him. He needs a life just as much as we do, and maybe not always with us." She gave Correk a tight hug. "We've been bad parents. Yumfuck has been building a place to have over a hundred of his closest friends so they'll want to come and play."

"A hundred!" Correk tried to let go and reach for the door but Leira wouldn't let him. "You are freakishly strong, woman," he said, as he heard a familiar "Wooooohooooo!" from inside the room.

"He must be trying out that kick ass slide," said Leira, pulling Correk away from the door. "Yumfuck has the right idea, you know. Mixed into all this hunting bad guys needs to be as much fun as possible."

"I know where we can start," said Correk, sliding a hand down the back of Leira's pants.

"You always say that, and it never gets old. Let's go on up to our own version of a fun house."

"I can build you a slide in our room if you think you need one," said Correk, following her up the stairs.

"You jest, but I'm thinking about it..."

"We have hundreds of years. It was bound to be suggested."

Leira laughed, pulling off her shirt at the top of the stairs and screaming with delight as Correk lifted her up and threw her toward the bed, shutting the door with his boot.

CHAPTER TWENTY-THREE

Wolfstan was dressed in his old clothes he had kept from Oriceran. Tall leather boots with buckles down the sides and suede pants. Leather straps that went around his chest and shoulders to hold in place a reinforced chest plate. *Today is not the time for stiff suits worn by tired businessmen.* He wanted to remember what it was like to be a proud Light Elf of Oriceran and stand in his leather armor when he unleashed his army for the first time on an unsuspecting public.

He had been in hiding since he had visited the sanctuary. Hastily piecing together something to replace his lost limb, licking his wounded pride. His rage was always at the surface now. Harder to keep in check. *Someone has to pay, and it won't be me.*

"Today is a good day, a very good day to crush their hopes and dreams to sand," he barked. His arms were bare, pockmarked by small scars everywhere, courtesy of the Willens and minor skirmishes from his days in Trevilsom. At the end of his right arm, where his hand used to be was a prosthetic made of gears and brown tanned cowhide shaped into a semblance of a hand. He flexed the hand, opening and shutting the coarse fingers. "I can still win the war, and then the battles will become meaningless. Chaos begets doubt, which leads to change. That creates new openings. It's not the most artful climb to power, but it'll do." He climbed to the top of the hill overlooking Key Bridge where it spilled into Rosslyn. It was just before rush hour, which never really ended in Washington D.C.

Behind him were four large moving trucks in a nearby parking lot with the emblem, Fleeker proudly displayed on the sides. He was done with trying to be subtle. "I tried to play nice, but you all shut the door on me. Well, I'm kicking the goddamn door open."

He raised his right arm and lowered it as the signal for his henchmen. They unlocked the back of the trucks and opened the doors, scurrying out of the way. Out piled the misshapen army of magicals dressed in black leather battle gear with guns locked into their prosthetics, freeing their hands. The twisted and glassy-eyed soldiers headed toward the highway and Key Bridge, one after the other, forming a battalion set loose in broad daylight among the humans.

"There's no going back now, my lovelies. Magic is out of the bottle. No Silver Griffins to stop me. Everyone running in different directions. No one will be able to put this one back in the bottle. Not even those bitches, Leira and Ariana."

He let out a low, menacing growl and watched with pleasure as the army crawled over cars like ants in dirt. Their orders were to do as much damage as possible but avoid taking lives. Wolfstan knew there was a line, and he wasn't ready to cross it just yet. "That's coming, but on my terms. First things first. Chaos with no sign of order returning any time soon."

It didn't take long for the news helicopters to circle overhead, filming cars being flipped and people hanging off the bridge, trying to get out of the way. Soldiers were throwing fireballs at abandoned cars setting them on fire and spraying bullets over people's heads. Wizards were casting spells turning metal into liquid that ran off the side of the bridge.

"Why let everyone else have all the fun?" roared Wolfstan, holding up his left hand and letting a fireball grow in size. He threw it at the nearest vehicle, a truck with side mirrors jutting out and chortled as it exploded, sending ashes high into the air.

A loud blast of sound erupted behind him. He watched as the minions dutifully stopped as the sound reached them. One by one, they turned and retreated back across the bridge toward Washington amid the wreckage and flames. Most of the bridge had emptied of humans except for a few hiding among what was left of their cars.

Once the soldiers reached the other side, they formed neat lines, piling back into the waiting trucks. Wolfstan waved to the helicopters still circling overhead as police cars and armored trucks finally arrived. But it was too late. Wolfstan had made his point and Light Elves stationed in black SUVs around the trucks easily fended off anyone trying to stop their departure.

"The age of magic has begun," said Wolfstan, feeling his anger settle back down just a little for the first time in weeks. "And it's gonna be a hell of a ride."

CHAPTER TWENTY-FOUR

Lois and Patsy stood outside the rebuilt gym on the grounds of the Virginia Seminary in Alexandria. "This was a good idea, Patsy. I'm glad we got to see this place again." She looked up at the new brick building, the black patent leather purse dangling on her arm.

"It's a nice reminder right about now that rebuilding is possible. Sometimes you even get a better building. I hear they put in saunas this time and a yoga room."

"Earl would love this," said Lois, pushing her glasses up her nose. "Really nice craftsmanship."

Patsy put her hand on her old friend's shoulder. "There is still a Silver Griffins and you're still in charge of them. We'd better start ambling up toward Aspinwall Hall. The Dean will be looking for us."

The two Witches made their way down the curving road that ran between the Seminary and the boys' boarding school on the other side of a chain link fence. "I like this time of year, especially in Virginia. The leaves are just starting to turn but there's a lot of green left." Patsy put her hand out as a maple leaf floated down from a tree. It landed in her open palm and she held onto it by the stem.

"An era is still over, Patsy. Magic has spilled out into the open and our agents are running for their lives. We're going to have to rethink how the Silver Griffins will operate. She held the purse closer as they went past the dormitories and up the hill by the library. The white tower of Aspinwall was visible through the trees where the road started to circle back around.

"The way I see it, we have a blank slate. It's a chance to figure out what worked really well and keep those things but ditch the rest." She dug around in her pocket and pulled out a tissue clinging to an old yellow peanut M&M. She pulled the two apart and inspected the M&M, finally popping it into her mouth, satisfied with its condition. "An obvious hole is what happened with Erickson. He had too much access too easily to too much information."

"Agreed. He's also slipped from our fingers and gone underground." Two students passed them, smiling and nodding as they made their way to the library.

"He'll emerge at some point and then we'll have him. I can't believe I'm going to say this, but a traitorous agent who exposed thousands of his peers may be the least of our problems right now."

Lois let out a sour laugh. "I'd say rescuing those who he might have harmed is paramount right now. Right after that is stopping Wolfstan Humphrey once and for all. But we can't afford to wait to rebuild the Silver Griffins, especially now that magic has been exposed. We need to set a precedent and establish it firmly. For that we will need a plan and finding Erickson will have to wait. I imagine wherever he is, remorse and regret are eating at him. He has a good family that he's cut off from and friends of his had to leave their lives and run. Perhaps that will be his punishment for now."

We could work on a multi-phase plan. Of course, we can figure out what we need to do right now to keep policing magicals and keep some kind of order. But take our time with the grander plan. Maybe reshape the Silver Griffins into an even better incarnation."

"General Anderson would be very proud of you right now."

"He's a human you can really admire. Must be a very busy day for him with magic's coming out party more of an opening salvo to war. That's gotta be a hard one to explain. I saw the fireballs going over the bridge. Woof!"

"I think a critical error we made with Wolfstan Humphrey was not perceiving clearly enough how far he is willing to go to create chaos. I've come to understand that he'd rather burn it all down with himself inside the flames, rather than lose. Now that I do get that it makes my resolve easier."

"Take him down, no matter what."

"I couldn't have said it any better," said Lois as they got to the doors of Aspinwall and went inside. The Dean was waiting for them in his office and got up from his desk to come around and greet the two Witches. "It seems we don't get the opportunity to meet under better circumstances very often. Perhaps that can change in the coming year," he said, shaking Lois' hand.

He sat on the edge of his large walnut desk, his cassock unbuttoned at the bottom over his dark grey slacks. "I understand we are to be honored with watching over the vault for the Silver Griffins. This is very unusual," he said, absently scratching the back of his greying short hair. "At first I thought you were asking for manpower to come and guard your Chicago vault, which seemed impractical."

"That is already being taken care of and involves lesser offensive artifacts. No, we need you to find a very safe place to leave this vault and tell no one. Hopefully, we will be back for it sooner rather than later." Lois slipped the purse off her arm and held it out for the Dean.

He took it from her, his hands gingerly wrapped around the edges as he held it away from his body. "It's so much lighter than I expected. You know, till now I'm not sure I ever thought about how magic could advance like a scientific discovery."

"Sometimes the two go hand in hand, like now. It's simple physics mixed with magic. Really quite obvious when you think about it," said Patsy, glancing around the spare office. "Where exactly are you planning to hide this very precious and dangerous item?"

"Not in this room, of course. There are too many people who come and go and not enough good hiding places. But there is a place in Richmond, a retreat center called Roslyn. It's one hundred and eighty-six acres of pristine land that runs along the James River. No one can enter or leave without being checked at the gate. But more importantly, the grounds hide their own secrets that are never revealed. I'm afraid that will have to include both of you. It's a rule we've had from the start in order to preserve the retreat."

Lois bit her lip, staring at the purse, but nodded. "In light of our recent transgression from one of our most trusted agents, I'm afraid I can't argue with your reasoning. There are care instructions that go along with your stewardship. There's a very large dragon that will need tending from time to time, and a few other creatures in the forest that was created."

The Dean's eyes grew wider and he gently placed the purse on his desk. "I didn't realize there would be wildlife care as well. Just how vast is this vault?"

"Far bigger than these grounds but smaller than a country," piped Patsy. "And there may be times we'll need access. Can that be arranged?"

"It would be difficult but could be arranged. Do so sparingly for the sake of the vault as well as those who have agreed to watch over it. Every time you come near, it will risk exposure, and therefore heighten the danger."

"Then we will consider carefully before a request is made and it will only come from me," said Lois. "If you hear from anyone else, consider it a ruse and take whatever actions you feel are necessary. The contents of that vault could upset the world more than anything else."

"More than your Wolfstan Humphrey?" The Dean wearily shook his head. "Yes, we've heard of him here, too. I saw the video of Key Bridge and I've heard through the briefings I get from our Order. He must be stopped."

"That's on our list," said Lois, taking off her glasses to wipe them with her cardigan. "Till we meet again and thank you. I really don't have the adequate words."

"It's part of our mission," said the Dean in a sober tone. "It's times like these that I'm actually grateful that we exist and have kept such a low profile. We are all glad to be of service."

Lois and Patsy walked out of the room, not looking back at the black patent leather purse that sat on the desk. The Dean closed the door behind them and within seconds they heard the familiar sound of sparks skittering across a wood floor as a portal was closing. The purse had already been moved.

"I guess it's on to agenda item number two," said Patsy. "We need to go help our fellow agents find a safe place to land."

"Let's get to it then. A new day has begun."

Marcy and Emmett got the signal that one of the magicals on their list was on the move. They were sitting in a booth by the large plate glass window in a diner on K Street. Their target was eating lunch at the fancier restaurant next door. "What's his bio say?" asked Emmett.

Marcy licked a finger and flipped a page. "His dossier says he's a corporate attorney and a Light Elf who is well known in political circles. Goes by the name of Leon Fitzgerald. Likely story."

"I'm not sure we're supposed to be evaluating his character, just keeping him alive and unharmed."

The phone on the table buzzed and Marcy picked it up, checking the GPS. "That is one fine spell Portia concocted." The tear drop displayed on the screen was moving. "Time to go," said Marcy, fitting the Nationals baseball cap on her head and slurping the rest of her tepid coffee. "You pay the bill and I'll go keep watch outside." She slid out of the booth and wove around a waitress carrying a piece of lemon meringue pie. "I will definitely have to come back here sometime," Marcy muttered as she pushed open the door and stepped in front of two men trying to get inside.

Marcy ignored the stares from them as she came out onto the broad sidewalk, scanning the area for the well-dressed tall man with slender features, typical of a Light Elf disguised with a glamour. "There you are, Leon. If that's really your name," whispered Marcy, stepping back closer to the diner window as the man stopped by the entrance to the restaurant next door. He was laughing and shaking hands with his two companions, quickly checking his watch.

"Did we catch him?" asked Emmett, as Marcy pointed at the cluster huddled near the door.

"He keeps checking his watch. Mr. Fitzgerald must have a meeting. We'll escort him back to his office and maybe go take a nice walk and do some early Christmas shopping."

"It's not even Halloween."

"I'm usually done by Halloween, you know that. That holiday has its own parties for our kind, and I like to really let loose. It's the only time of the year when the veil becomes thin and I'm always hoping for a visit from my Aunt June."

"She's the one who died in her new vibrating recliner, right?"

"The same. Okay, he's on the move. Kiss me Emmett." Marcy put her hands on Emmett's cheeks, pulling him closer as the Light Elf glided by, not noticing them.

"What was that for? Not that I'm complaining."

"I didn't want him to notice us. It worked, didn't it?"

"Sure, if you say so. Totally necessary. Come on, let's get

after him." He took Marcy's hand and they started walking, keeping half a block between them and Leon Fitzgerald who was striding confidently down the sidewalk toward his destination.

A burly figure wrapped up in a dark green wool coat too warm for the day brushed past Marcy, knocking her in the shoulder with a grunt. "Scuse you," retorted Marcy, scowling at his retreating back. "Some people."

Emmett watched the man stomp past a few other people and felt a hum across the back of his neck. "I think it's operation go time, Marcy." He pulled his hand away from Marcy and felt the flickers of a fireball forming as he picked up his pace. "Call the others."

"What are you talking about? I don't see anything. You mean that oaf? He's just a rude... wait a minute."

The large man stood up straighter, revealing a Kilomea not bothering with a glamour. Tusks jutted from his mouth and fur was growing along his face and neck. "Holy crap!" Marcy pulled out her phone, almost dropping it and quickly texted the others. "Only Portia and George are close enough to do anything." She dug around in her pocket, fumbling for the piece of paper with the spell on it. "Two moons! I checked and doublechecked," she said, exasperated as her fingers finally closed around the slightly crumpled note. She pulled it out and read the spell again even though she had it memorized.

The Kilomea had already clamped his hands down on the shoulders of the surprised Leon Fitzgerald. He was lifting him up, over his head and was ready to carry him away. Everyone around them was scattering. A Gnome let out a squeal of horror but collected himself and did a fairly decent job of biting the Kilomea's leg before he was shaken off and kicked for good measure.

"Ollie, ollie, oxen free to this spot you shall see. Come as close as this may be." Marcy moved her hands in the shapes that Leira and Correk had carefully shown them.

"Is that it?" asked Emmett. "You think it worked?"

A strong gust of wind blew down the sidewalk, almost knocking Marcy to her knees. The wind swirled around the Kilomea and his prize as Correk appeared from inside the maelstrom, grabbing onto the Kilomea and disappearing back into the swirl of wind just as quickly. Leon Fitzgerald suddenly found himself falling seven feet to the ground, knocking the wind out of him. He lay on his side gasping for air as Marcy and Emmett rushed to him. "Are you okay? Can you sit up?" asked Marcy as Emmett helped him get onto his feet. "Nothing seems broken."

George and Portia came running around the corner breathless and wide-eyed. "Did we make it in time?" asked Portia.

"Where's the fire?" George looked around at the frightened faces still hugging the wall of a nearby GAP store. "We clearly missed something," he said, looking for any signs of trouble.

"You should have seen it," said an excited Marcy. "I did the spell just like they said and *poof*! Out of nowhere a wind came up and Correk was there," she said, pointing, "and then he wasn't."

"He sucked a decent-sized Kilomea away with him. That has to be three hundred pounds, easy. I could never handle being a Fixer," said Emmett, still helping Leon stay on his feet.

"What the hell was that?" Leon choked out the words.

"Your luckiest day ever," said George, gently patting him on the back.

Portia looked around at all the frightened faces. "Do we even try never was, never will be?"

"Your guess is as good as mine," said Marcy. "Things changed like someone flipped a switch. Maybe they're safer if they do know that magic is real."

CHAPTER TWENTY-FIVE

Correk gave into the spell, spinning through two places for a moment with an angry companion. They stopped rotating as images took shape around them. The Kilomea immediately started swinging, trying to hit anything, but it was pointless.

Turner Underwood easily leaned back, his hands still on his cane and his bowler undisturbed. "You, sir, are in the depths of my house. Well, one of my houses."

"The Fixer," gasped the Kilomea.

"Emeritus," said Turner. "You are currently in the grasp of my successor. Where was I?" Turner pointed a finger in the air as the Kilomea continued to grunt and growl, his hands curled into fists. "There's very little magical reception down here. Unless you're a Fixer and know what you're doing at a much higher level. No one will hear you and no one will ever know what became of you."

Droplets of sweat formed on the fur along the Kilomea's face but he gave off no sign of panic.

"I suppose that is a lot like the proposition you had for

the Light Elf you were intent on grabbing. Funny how life changes on a dime sometimes. Have a seat, sir. You and I are going to chat about everything you know when it comes to Wolfstan Humphrey." Turner made a show of sitting on a carved wooden chair with a high back that resembled a throne. Behind the Kilomea was brown metal folding chair cold to the touch. "Before you consider protesting, keep in mind that there are no rules down here except mine. Choose not to speak and you stay down here in this box even if it's hundreds of years. I have enough boxes just like this that I don't care. And after what you were willing to do to a fellow magical, I no longer have any compassion either."

Correk's cheek twitched. He couldn't tell if Turner meant what he said or if that was a fitting punishment. But a sudden shift in the magical stream tugged at his attention, distracting him from Turner's inquisition. "I have to go. Despite the world being turned on its end, there's still more mundane tasks to attend."

"Go," said Turner, with a wave of his hand. "We will be fine. Well, I will at least. Whether or not my friend here is will be entirely up to him. Tell me, sir, did you witness when they butchered a magical and tore out his organs? Did you hold them down?"

Correk saw the flash of panic in the Kilomea's eyes just before he swept out of there. *Maybe Turner is right.*

Correk found himself in a dressing room of a Wal-Mart in Grand Rapids, Michigan. He opened the louvered door and walked out into the store looking for the distress call. "How many items did you have?" asked a bored, pale young woman in a matching powder blue sweater set and tan slacks. She was scrolling through her phone watching Tik Tok videos, not even looking up at Correk.

"None," said Correk. "Just passing through."

"Through the dressing room? Come on, dude. Don't make me call security." She glanced at Correk, distracted and went back to her phone. "They already have their hands full. Some lady is trying to steal the store. Not too bright."

"I'm telling you, I didn't do it." Correk could hear the loud pleas of the Light Elf who was in trouble. The trail of magic swirled around the store before piling up in one glittery direction. He quickly made his way toward the front of the store and the exit. He came around a tall display of cooking pans and saw a young mother with a cart surrounded by two officers. In the seat of the cart was a toddler with dark wavy hair, smiling and clapping his hands, turning his head to listen to whoever was yelling at any given moment.

The mother had her hands open wide and was pleading as she gestured at the large pile next to her. "I didn't put those things anywhere. They're not mine."

"Ma'am, we found them next to your car. Who else would leave you toys like that right outside your minivan?"

"It's a little off Santa's beat, don't you think?" asked the shorter officer.

Shoppers exited the store, craning their necks as they passed trying to get a better look. A woman pushed a large Fischer Price box with a colorful image of a Launch and

Loop Raceway on the side, struggling to get it out of the store. The toddler's mouth pursed with delight as he watched it pass and he squeezed his palms together. Correk watched with amusement as the little boy's eyes glowed and his cheeks reddened. "This should be fun," muttered Correk.

The raceway disappeared with a *pop* out of the woman's cart and reappeared with another *pop* just behind the officer, almost tripping him.

"Hey, who took my toy!" yelled the woman, turning around in a circle, her forehead wrinkled in confusion.

"How did that get here?" asked the taller officer with a shiny bald head. "Did you put that there?" he said, scowling at the young mother.

"How would I do that with you standing right next to me?" she asked, while simultaneously trying to pull her son's hands apart and telling him, "No, Jeffrey. That's not yours. Remember we talked about this. We buy things."

The shorter cop laughed. "She's trying to say the baby took the stuff," he said, shaking his head.

What did Turner always say? Pick the route of least resistance. Correk snapped his fingers, setting off car alarms in a pattern across the parking lot. Wave after wave of noise as one car started and then another. Shoppers piled out of the Wal-Mart, running to their cars as the woman with a cart continued to protest about her missing toy. He swirled a finger overhead and created a sound barrier around the toddler, who smiled and pointed to Correk.

"That kid is going to be trouble when he gets older.

Already smarter than the adults around him," said Correk, giving the boy a small wave.

The bald cop pressed his hands to his ears and shouted. "You better call for backup."

"For what, exactly?" shouted his partner. "And who are we arresting? The cars in the parking lot?"

"There it is." The woman made her way over and scooped up the toy, tsking at the officers as she put it back in her cart, pushing it through the crowd of people still pushing out of the store. Others were gathering to see what was happening and pulling out their phones to film it.

Correk slipped past the crowds and whispered in the shorter officer's ear. "Go back in the store. This is done." The cop walked away with his partner yelling behind him. "Hey, where are you going, Phil?" He looked at the woman and at the pile of merchandise. "Wait here," he said in a stern voice.

Correk took her by the arm and pushed the cart into the parking lot. "Where's your car?" he said into a sound tunnel.

The woman's eyes widened, and she blinked past tears. "Right over there," she said, pointing to a maroon minivan.

"Leave the little fellow at home the next time," said Correk, smiling at the small boy. "Consider getting him a tutor from an Oriceran teacher. Sooner rather than later." He chucked the little boy under the chin and crossed his eyes for him, eliciting a squeal of delight. "Maybe one of these would be nice."

The Light Elf arched an eyebrow as she pulled the little boy out of the shopping cart. "Careful or you'll catch baby fever and before you know it, you're trying to explain away portaling toys across a parking lot." She sat the boy in his car seat, strapping him in. "You're a Light Elf too, right? Hundreds of years of parenting. Just keep that in mind. It literally never ends."

Correk waited till they pulled out of the parking lot safely and then he snapped his fingers again and the noise stopped. There were people dotted here and there who had been fidgeting with cars and trucks or holding up their phones. All of them stopped and looked around, startled by the quiet. "Just another day at the office," said Correk as he walked away, looking for a good spot to travel home.

CHAPTER TWENTY-SIX

"Is that you?" Leira poked her head out of the living room. Correk was stepping through a portal, a smile lingering on his face. "I thought you were on a mission. Things go that well? What's with the goofy grin?" asked Leira.

"You ever think your mother was right? Maybe we should think about a kid."

"What exactly happened on that mission? You do know the world has just been turned upside down. Let's table that for a second."

"We'll talk about it later."

Leira drew her head back and took a longer look. "Yeah, okay, we can do that. Do male Elves have some kind of internal clock?"

"Now who's not making sense."

"Never mind, we'll find a nice table for two when the world rights itself just a little and figure out children. Wow, that sounded weird just saying it." She stepped back into the living room, calling to him. "For now, try and hold on to that good feeling when you come in here." She was holding the TV remote in one hand and watching the news. "This is the Feds answer to what happened on Key Bridge. I guess they agree with Wolfstan on some levels. Too late to deny anymore and might as well start talking about magic. Control the narrative."

Correk came and stood next to her, his hands on his hips. "This is what they start with? A report on trolls. You know what's coming..." Images of Yumfuck riding a bull, and then dancing on a stage at Comicon, and then swimming around in the Reflecting Pool with Nibbler flashed across the screen.

"At least they don't have his name." Leira let out a sigh. "This is not going to distract anyone from fire and mayhem."

"Especially when the public eventually figures out a five inch troll can become an eight foot warrior."

"General Anderson said they're going to try the comic book approach next. Walk out magical superheroes who are supposed to protect everyone. Make a big show of catching the bad guys. He said it would take a few days to assemble a few new qualified bounty hunters and set them loose. Elves are their first choice for casting. Apparently, I made a good impression. Wood or Light Elves are wanted for publicity, but I declined the spotlight for both of us."

"Thank you, much appreciated. This could all go very badly, very quickly."

Leira clicked it off. "There's already a few tremors. Some cities have curfews and toilet paper is hard to find. Not sure how that will fight off an angry Gnome intent on pillaging."

"Do we have enough?"

Leira gave him a crooked smile. "We have plenty and thank you. I needed that reminder that we still have a life right here in this house. Matthew and Angel are stuck at the hospital. Humans are expecting the worst, I guess. I said we'd keep an eye on their house, just in case." Leira looked up at the ceiling. "I wonder if this is what it was like the last time magic was brought back. Maybe it's like this every time and the beginning is just gonna be a rough landing. I remember what it was like for me when I first found out. Confusing, scary. And there was nothing blowing up or catching on fire."

"Just a hungry troll and a murder to solve."

"That sounds so benign right about now. We have really gone a long way down this rabbit hole." Leira's phone pinged and she pulled it out, reading the text. "Ariana wants us to come to her estate. She said it's urgent and useful. Very cryptic of her."

"I don't see how we say no. Let's bring the troll."

"Our family celebrity. She sent exact coordinates that are inside her wards. Something big must be happening."

"Or dangerous. It's still the dark families. We go ready to battle. It wasn't that long ago we fought our way out of there." Correk strapped on his bow and a quiver of arrows.

"Ariana showed me another side to the place. It's possible she wants to help. Wolfstan has a way of uniting enemies." Leira put two fingers in her mouth and whistled for Yumfuck. He came running out of his room and leaped onto the banister, sliding down on his feet. He was wearing his cape and mask and had his hands on his hips. "I am Batfuck, at your service. What's the problem, ma'am?"

"Leave the mask and cape this time. We're heading into bigger trouble and I'm gonna need the eight foot version of you to be ready at a moment's notice."

Yumfuck reluctantly took off his outfit and carefully folded each item, leaving them on the banister.

"Let's make a family pact." Leira looked around at the house and the pictures of family lined up on a table. "We may be heading into harder times that pull us away from each other for longer stretches. Let's promise we remember to check back in on a daily basis." The troll put out his fist. "Wait, not done," said Leira. "We will have to be the ones to remind each other that we have a life. A real life full of laughter and friends and hanging out with each other just having a beer on the back porch. Once in a while, each of us may forget that and it's going to take this promise, this pact we make right here to keep us together like we are right now."

"Leira, do you really think things could get to be that bad?"

"It's a possibility and I want to be sure when we're out there trying to save some little corner of the world that back here, there's still the real us. Our family. Promise me, and each other. If we see that one of us is getting lost out there to the fight, we pull them back to this space. We will remember this moment just before it all started."

"I love you, Leira, for a hundred years and more."

Leira reached out and took Correk's hand. "Till the end of time. I never even knew there was love like this till there was you."

"I love you both," squeaked the troll, rubbing his eyes.

"Our first kid, kind of," said Leira holding out her other

hand for his paw. Correk completed the circle, taking Yumfuck's other paw and they stood there, the last light of the day streaming in through the window by the front door. "This is our family, and we will fight our way through hell to protect what we have."

"We will keep this love in our hearts," said the troll, "and carry it into every battle."

"If it's the last good thing that we do," said Leira, taking in every moment, trying to memorize it and burn it in her mind. "Okay, then it begins. Let's portal out of here and find out what good thing Ariana has for us. A new world order has started. Let's go embrace it."

CHAPTER TWENTY-SEVEN

The portal opened just inside the barn where Leira had faced down Sirius and watched as shifters streamed past her into the woods. She felt the echo of those days as she let the magic drift into her feet, crawling up her spine, her eyes beginning to glow. The troll stood on her shoulder, holding onto her collar. Correk was behind her, keeping watch in the other direction.

"I can't say I blame you." Ariana came out of the shadows with her hands up to show they were empty of any wand. "We are in strange and dangerous times that grow more so by the day." She stepped out under a light bulb, casting shadows on her striking features. She was dressed in jeans and a tight black turtleneck, with tall riding boots. Uncle Felix walked out next to her dressed in a natty dark suit, a white collared shirt open at the neck. The corners of his mouth were curling up ever so slightly. "Good evening fellow magicals. Love the bow and arrows look." He ran his hands down in front of his body and struck a pose. "This is battle gear for anyone in the Dark Families. We have a certain style reputation to keep."

"Can it, Uncle. Save the schtick for a later date when the world is at a seven on the danger scale instead of a full ten with flying monkeys." Ariana came closer. "What Wolfstan is doing to our kind is unforgivable." Her expression turned stony. "Enough trying to put out these fires. We need to bring the fight to him and wipe him off the face of two worlds."

"None of this is news, Ariana. Please tell me you didn't bring us all this way to make announcements." Leira stared back at her, trying to gauge whether they were still friends, or slipping into foes.

Ariana cocked her head to one side. "You don't trust me, even now. I'd be the same way. Respect. Then let's do a show and tell, with more of the show portion. That's the only way you'll understand we're on the same side."

"At least for now," said Uncle Felix, smiling. "Wait till you see the surprise." He fanned his hands out by his face. "Kaboom. It will blow your minds."

"Why does that sound creepy when you say it," said Leira.

"Aloha motherfucker," said the troll, eyeing Uncle Felix suspiciously.

"Oh yeah," said Correk. "Hello *or* goodbye."

"You, I like," said Uncle Felix, pointing at the troll.

They walked out of the barn to a golf cart waiting by the gravel road. "We're riding over that hill. Leira you get up front with me. Uncle Felix if you're coming you have to ride in the back with Correk."

Uncle Felix reluctantly followed the others to the black

golf cart with lights strung around the top. He sat down on the bench seat and grabbed the bar next to his head. "Seems like kind of a letdown to be chugging over the hillside in a golf cart, doesn't it? I mean, come on, a portal would have added nicely to the gravitas."

Leira bit her lip sitting in the front, trying not to smile as Correk arched a brow and shifted his bow, wedging it between himself and the Wizard.

They rode over the hill, the light shining in their eyes. Leira put up her hand as shade as they crested the top. The land opened up in front of her for miles to the west and north in green fields of Kentucky. Ariana stopped the cart and waved to a Witch far below.

Leira half stood out of her seat, holding on to the cart and dropped her hand. "Correk..."

Correk half turned in his seat, ignoring the satisfied grin on Uncle Felix's face.

In front of them, across the green fields were hundreds and hundreds of magicals assembling into groups. Portals were still opening on every side, depositing even more Elves and Gnomes, Witches and Dwarves, Crystals and even Kilomeas and Atlanteans. "Every kind of magical is here," said Ariana. "Including most of my family from every corner of the world."

In the center of the group were hundreds of Witches and Wizards all dressed in black. "The Dark Families," said Uncle Felix. "We do make a statement. It's our branding."

Large white tents had been erected on the southern side near the trees with cots and refreshments and places to meet and draw up battle plans. Some of the Witches and Wizards were directing magicals to different places.

"I called in a few favors," said Ariana. "The Dark Families have ties that run deep with Oriceran and once everyone understood what was at stake, they started showing up in droves. The portals have been opening since early this morning. It's been the same with magicals here on Earth. So many of them know of someone who has disappeared. They all want to fight back and get the chance to rescue their friends."

"Why didn't you at least tell the Fixer, first?"

"Remember how wary you were just being here? I believe an associate of yours has even joined the fun. My cousin, Freda called him."

Leira followed the direction Ariana was pointing and saw a tall Wizard with blonde curly hair standing next to a short, dark haired Gnome. "Louie... Louie is here, Correk."

"Of course he is," said Uncle Felix. "He's an honorary member of the Dark Families. His mother on Oriceran is one of us."

Ariana glared at her uncle who opened his mouth in mock surprise. "This day is just full of surprises."

"You knew about Louie's connection to you, and to me, and didn't tell me." Leira watched Louie as he helped people step out of a portal. "Are those human beings coming through a portal? What is happening?"

"It wasn't my secret to tell and besides, Louie hasn't had much contact with his family for a very long time. The only time he's set foot on this land since he was a small child was to defend you, Leira. It's pretty clear where his loyalties lie." Ariana stepped out of the cart and stood on the hill, her hands on her hips. "Now, those humans down below. Those are not ordinary people." She smiled, waving her arm high overhead to get Louie's attention. "You are looking at what have to be your cousins, Leira. Each of them is pure, one hundred percent special and possess the spark of humanity in its full dosage."

Leira stepped out and stood on the firm ground. Energy was buzzing up and down her spine and the old scar on her belly was tingling. She opened and closed her hands feeling her heartbeat pick up.

"Our secret weapon," said Uncle Felix. "They can suggest a change of heart into someone's mind, particularly the vulnerable. Our zombie brethren fit that bill perfectly."

"Leira, didn't you ever notice how easily you inspire others? That piece of you that's the spark of humanity carries some weight." Ariana walked back to the cart and pulled out her wand from under the seat. "It was always nearby," she said, with a wink. "I have issues with trust as well." She raised her wand over the valley and tapped it twice, sending a loud crack over the heads of everyone below. All the magicals turned to look up the hill as Leira started running down, not waiting to see what would happen next.

She had spotted someone familiar standing next to Louie.

"Dad, you're here!" She picked up speed with the troll holding on tight on her shoulder, as her legs moved faster, easily navigating the grassy hill. She ran into his arms as he lifted her off her feet, hugging her tight. "Of course I'm here. The call went out for help. It helps that Louie came to my cabin and dragged my ass here," he said, putting Leira down and kissing her head. Nibbler crawled out of his pocket and waved to Yumfuck who trilled.

Louie ran his hand through his curly hair, grinning. "Hello, Leira. I brought a few friends with me to the party." He was standing next to Ava, his sword strapped to his back. Ronnie was busy helping the last of the people through the open portal. Mr. Hou was quietly directing the Order into straight lines, facing Leira.

Magicals covered the entire field and were moving around Leira to get to different tents or say hello to someone they recognized. Correk finally caught up with Leira, putting his arm around her shoulders. "There hasn't been a gathering of magicals like this since we fought Rhazdon and her followers hundreds of years ago," he said, excited.

"We are a part of this family that has been woven together," said Leira, awe in her voice. "I've never felt the connection as much as right now."

"We meet again?" Leira turned and found Katie standing in front of her, the glamour dropped for the moment and her hair replaced by dark, writhing snakes. "Our paths keep crossing?"

"Katie, you've joined the fray. I thought you were strictly on board for paying gigs."

"Everyone has a place where money no longer matters. Wolfstan Humphrey has found it for about a thousand magicals who wouldn't say hello to each other on any other day. Hell, a few of them would bite some of them and stew them for dinner?"

"What about the Silver Griffins? They should be here, too. What's left of them."

"They're invited." Ariana had pulled up the cart and was stepping out of it. "Lois is a cousin of mine too. Sirius was her brother. They are gathering as many Silver Griffin agents as they can to meet us at the battlefield. Wolfstan's hidden base. Someone was able to crack someone on the inside."

Jackson tightened the leather ties on the long knife strapped to his leg. "Turner Underwood, of course. I hear it wasn't pretty, but he got what we needed."

Leira glanced up at Correk but his expression was stony, and he was making a point of looking out over the field of magicals.

Crack!

A portal opened at the front of the crowd, spraying the grass with bronze sparks. A quiet immediately rolled over the crowd as the King of Oriceran and Queen Saria stepped through the portal. Behind them was Lucius and the Old King of Oriceran, accompanied by Queen Azure of the Virgo Kingdom, and the ruling council of Dwarves that lived in the mountains.

The Old King clapped his hand on his son's shoulder. "We are reunited. At long last."

"Another intercession by Turner Underwood," whispered Correk. "It was past due."

"That had to have been a mixed reaction." Leira nodded to the Queen who lifted her chin but gave a slight nod of respect as well.

"For so many reasons," said Correk. "Where's Harkin?" he asked, craning his neck but couldn't find the familiar figure of his tall father.

"Turner Underwood asked him to stay behind and get the machines ready," said Lucius. "Harkin and Lily have been working day and night to replicate them. The refugees from Turner's house have been helping. It's taken everyone from that strange city of his to build them and gather enough shifter blood to make this plan work."

"You'll see him soon enough," said the King. "I look forward to speaking with him as well. It's been too long."

"Even Peyton is helping," said Queen Saria, giving away nothing. Her mind was already on the battle ahead. She was wearing a silver crown that held purple sprouts. The sign of death that was yet to come. She was dressed in a smaller version of leather battle gear and tall boots, wielding a broadsword with an 'O' engraved at the hilt.

Lucius came and stood beside the royals, towering over most of them. "The shifters are gathering at the battle site. We've gotten as many of them together as we could find." He was grinning and beating a fist on his chest. "It's a good day to test our mettle."

"Lucius seems in his element," said Leira.

"I've heard stories about what he was like when he was young. If he wasn't in a battle, he was in a fight."

"Do you think we're ready for Wolfstan? Even with all this, I wonder if he doesn't have a few surprises left for us. It seems like he's always a step ahead."

Correk pulled his braid out from under his bow. "I know that we are going into battle with everything we have and that's all that can be asked of us. Whatever happens, we'll know we did our part to save our worlds from his grand plans."

"Then let's get started. We need to move all these resources to another location."

"That's where we come into the picture," said Queen Saria, interrupting them. "Our magic is known to be stronger in this world than most. We can open larger portals and keep them stable long enough for everyone to quickly move onto the battlefield."

Ariana came and stood in the center of the royals and Leira and Correk. "We are off to a small southwest Texas town. Terlingua, Texas in Brewster County near the Rio Grande. Humans call it a ghost town inhabited by dead miners. Magicals believe the entire town is a thin place where those who are trapped in the world in between can almost reach out and touch you. At least that's the legend. It's the perfect place to hide an army because no one is looking and most stay away."

"We are bound to trip his wards," said the King of Oriceran standing next to his father. "Queen Azure is particularly adept at destroying them and will go ahead of us to work her magic."

"We have worked out a landing strategy that has been shared with the shifters and the Silver Griffins," said the Old King, unfolding his hands as colorful dots and dashes leapt from his fingertips, forming a topographical map that hung in the air. "This is Terlingua and these," he said, moving his hands in different directions as small blue dots appeared to the south, "are the shifters." Orange dots appeared to the north. "This will be the Silver Griffins. These black dots are our troops moving straight down the middle. Turner Underwood will be waiting to guide the humans and help them manipulate the altered magicals. But Wolfstan has his own paid army to back them up and keep them in line."

"We sent scouts," said Lucius, "and they are stationed mostly to this side," he said pointing up at the map.

"Everyone here has been prepped, except for you two," said the King. "Leira and Correk, you are to lead the second wave where we expect to be hit the hardest. Wolfstan will try his magical army first, hoping that does us in. If the spark of humanity works and we can slow them down or even stop them, he'll catch on quickly and send in his paid recruits. Then the real fighting begins. Are you ready?"

"Son," said the old King. "Lead us off."

The King of Oriceran lifted his sword high into the air and yelled, "Today, we fight with honor..."

A chorus went up that joined in his battle cry. "And to the end!"

Leira took Correk's hand and squeezed it. "If it's the last good thing we do." Correk leaned down and kissed her, mashing her lips and lingering for a moment. "We make sure we get back to that little house and our lives," he said, touching his forehead to hers.

"Then we can talk about everything," she said with a crooked smile. "I love you."

"Always and forever," he replied, as Queen Saria opened the first portal.

Pearson Cowley barged into Fleeker, pushing aside guards with a simple display of magic that overwhelmed everyone long enough to gain access without bloodshed. Silver Griffin agents quickly moved in with him to remove the guards and take their place, taking control of the building and the eighth floor. Agents made their way to the eighth floor to shut down the labs and secure information. They slowed down when they saw the animals who had been altered. Some had to step outside for some air, while others grew more determined to stop Wolfstan Humphrey as they arrested everyone on that floor.

Pearson pushed past Wolfstan's assistant, barking, "You're fired," as he made his way to Wolfstan's suite and the meeting room. He sat down at the top of the long, mahogany table in Fleeker headquarters, waiting for the guests who had been quickly gathered and were being escorted into the building. Soon enough, he was surrounded at the table by other board members from Fleeker and Axiom and conglomerates from all over the world.

"I've called this meeting in light of what we've all seen on the news," said Pearson, laying his wand down on the table. Several of the board members look surprised and sat back in their chairs. Others leaned forward, interested to hear what he said next.

"Wolfstan Humphrey has become a menace that will be crushed under a force that has never been marshalled before on this world. If he is seen as still in charge of this company, because of our agreement across several corporations, we will be crushed with him. We have a majority in session here," he said, with a nod. "I move that he is removed from his position as chairman of Fleeker and fired from any active position, effective immediately."

"I second it," said an older woman sitting at the far end. "And with relish."

"All in favor?"

Every hand was raised, even if some came up more

slowly than others. "Then the motion carries. If anyone in this room is found to still be associating with Wolfstan Humphrey after this meeting," said Pearson, "let me assure you, we will find out and you will be dealt with harshly. The age of Wolfstan Humphrey is over today. A new age where magic and technology are used for the good of all has begun."

CHAPTER TWENTY-EIGHT

Wolfstan Humphrey sat in his bunker under the hard soil of Terlingua, Texas contemplating his next move. He knew they were coming for him. He had seen it all in the magical plate before it was destroyed and became a pile of sand. Every time he had poured the water and blew softly across the top, he had seen the images of magicals pouring over the ground. But the ending was hidden from him each time no matter how he asked the question.

He pounded his fist against the hard, earthen wall. "No matter," he growled. "I'm ready. Bring everything you have to bear into my world. Let's see if you can best me." He heard the commotion overhead and knew the fight had begun. "Time to pay the piper," he sneered, as he rose and made his way down a narrow, damp hallway to a metal ladder that led outside to the battle. Black mist swirled around his feet, crawling up his legs as he climbed.

His lieutenants had been given the exact time the opposition would arrive. Wolfstan knew that much from what he had seen in the plate. His armies were ready and positioned to fight them off. But after that, the plate had become murky and showed nothing further. "I am left to the mercy of fate." He put his remaining hand against the metal plate at the top and took a deep breath, pushing the covering aside and rising above the ground, far enough back from the main fighting, for now.

He had positioned himself perfectly to see the show he knew was coming. When the plate had failed to tell him the ending, Wolfstan had done what he always did. He went looking for a Plan B that would tilt things in his direction. It was no matter to him that the cost might turn out to be high for both sides. If the others were defeated then he could pay his debt knowing he had won, at last. He would have their twisted respect and two worlds would know that they should have welcome him into their circles when they had the chance. "Too late," he sullenly muttered, as the black swirl followed him, curling around his heavy boots that went well past his knees. He climbed atop a metal structure to get a better view across the endlessly flat ground.

He looked with fatherly pride at the army he had created. Long lines of magicals bearing the scars of artifacts embedded in their bodies making them stronger, giving them more endurance. Their eyes were generally glassy, and they took their positions, facing out from two large arcs.

The air surrounding the expanse began to crackle and shimmer.

Boom! Boom! Boom!

Wolfstan pulled a silver flask out of his pocket and

unscrewed the top clumsily with his left hand, annoyed. He took a long swig before raising it up in a toast. "Today is a good day to kick everyone's ass."

Enormous portals began to open, sparks catching the grass on fire as Queen Azure stepped through, swinging her wand from side to side in large arcs. Silver rain began to fall from a clear sky, lighting up the wards that dissolved just as quickly as they became opaque. The magical rain grew, covering the field, leaving glittering snow on the ground that crunched underfoot.

Magicals from Oriceran poured out of the opening next and onto the waiting ground. Silver Griffin agents appeared to their left with Lois and Patsy at the front. On the other side, large wolves gathered, howling in unison. Lucius came through the portal and raised his sword, howling louder than any of them. The wolves answered him and streamed down the hill toward the army, boxing them in. Wolfstan's zombie army threw fireballs at the shifters, wounding a large grey wolf who ran to the back, yipping as the smell of burnt hair filled the air. But the others shifted to the left and the right, avoiding the fire, nipping at their opponents. A soldier lifted a sword, ready to slice at a wolf but was stopped by a large brown female shifter who leapt onto him. She stood on his chest and bit his arm hard enough to make him drop the sword, leaving him with a flesh wound. She growled in his face, drool sliding onto his face but did nothing more, running off to rejoin her pack.

The commands were very clear on that point. No one was to strike a deadly blow unless absolutely necessary.

Katie stood with the few Atlanteans who had answered

the call, stretching her bow and firing off an arrow that barely missed its mark, startling the soldier who ran toward her.

The noise was deafening. Soldiers faces were twisted in pain and rage, coming at the Silver Griffins, firing off a spray of bullets. But the agents were all veterans who had faced red tides that could dissolve a magical and monsters that could fly with claws to tear apart flesh. They held up their wands, creating shields to deflect the rounds as the second wave behind them cast a spell to send out a surge of energy that pushed the army in the direction of the portals.

"Is this a tactic or are they already losing?" Wolfstan pulled out binoculars and watched with amusement.

Witches from the Dark Families came through the portal with their wands raised, creating a shield. They marched forward, dressed all in black but stopped short, letting the soldiers advance. Wolfstan's brow furrowed but he watched intently, wondering when someone would finally strike down one of his own soldiers and live with regret or give up their own life. The prospect made him howl with glee.

Louie came through the portal next surrounded by the humans with Ava and Mr. Hou by his side. They spread out in a straight line, making no attempt to move forward, stretching out along the flat land as one by one they took their spot.

"Now what?" Wolfstan stood up in his chair, the fingers of his prosthetic responding to his surprise and sudden rage, curling together in a fist, bending the metal supports on the railing in front of him. He looked through the binoculars and watched with curiosity, even as the dark mist tipped over the edge of his viewing stand, inching forward.

The humans took each other's hand, forming a solid line and focused on the magicals in front of them, sending out one unified thought that had been decided back in Kentucky.

Give peace a chance. You're among friends. We can help you.

They sent the message out in a loop, over and over again, letting the suggestion sink into the deepest part of the tortured magicals. The soldiers pressed forward, getting closer to the humans. Louie tried to step off the line, his sword in his hand. *Stay where you are*, the sword whispered to him and he stepped back, watching them get closer.

Slowly, the noise ebbed and the soldiers on the field looked around in confusion. The shifters pushed closer, growling and barking to herd the army toward the humans. The soldiers marched slowly as if they were in a stupor. The Witches parted, letting them pass and then the line of human being made a path for them, stepping back.

"No! No, no, no!" cried Wolfstan, shaking his prosthetic hand in the air.

Crack! A large portal opened and on the other side Turner Underwood was waiting with his daughter, Winland at his side. Harkin and Lily stood on the other side of the portal, waiting patiently for the soldiers to make their way into the Texas sanctuary. The human beings were the last to go through the portal, leaving the battle-field. Louie hugged Ava tight and pushed her through, even as she tried to resist. "You aren't used to having to fight for your life."

"But what about you? I just found you."

"There's so many bad dates ahead of us. I'll even let you win the next time we train."

Ava smiled even as a tear rolled down her face and she brushed it away. "I'll beat you fair and square, and we both know it."

"Very true," he said, kissing her even as Mr. Hou grumbled. "Well, maybe just this once," her father muttered.

Louie let go and pushed her through the portal, looking at her face till it finally closed, leaving burn marks along the ground.

"Phase one went off with only minor injuries," said Lois, pushing her glasses up her nose. They were retreating back to their earlier positions.

"Yeah, but we both know that was just the appetizer. I'm pretty sure the main course is about to be served. Now we aim to kill, and so do they."

The ground shook as Lois reached out to steady her friend. "I think we're starting phase two. Buckle up."

"Let's get a pizza when this is done," said Patsy, a grim smile on her face. "That would be something worth winning for."

"Okay, but no pineapple this time."

"We'll get two."

The ground shook again and peeled back a large section in the middle catching a few of the Witches from the Dark Families off guard. They slid toward the deep hole that was made, swinging their wands to try and create a spell and catch themselves. A dark haired Wizard went over the edge, his eyes wild with panic and disappeared below the surface with a scream.

But that was soon muffled by the rumble of a thousand feet climbing the stone stairs that appeared in the enormous hole.

Boom! Boom! Boom!

One large portal opened and Leira Berens stepped through with Correk by her side. Her eyes were glowing and the symbols along her arms were flipping over rapidly. A fireball already rested in her open hand. "Today, we fight to finish it."

Yumfuck dropped off her shoulder, scrambling to the ground where he grew to eight feet tall. He let out a roar that showed all of his large, sharp teeth, and flexing his arms.

Jackson stepped up next to Leira and set Nibbler on the ground. He stood back as Nibbler grew to his full height and went to stand next to his friend as they roared again, this time in unison. Magicals stepped up behind Leira crowding the space. She took a look back at the hundreds of faces and raised her fist in the air. A cheer arose as she faced forward and marched toward the opening in the ground.

Magicals came up the stairs, ready to fight. "Wolfstan's paid army," growled Correk. "It looks like we fight our own kind after all, today. But at least they deserve the ending that's coming for them."

Elves and Witches and Crystals and every other creature ran past Leira, pouring through the portal that stretched out for two hundred feet. Leira smiled up at Correk and said, "I love you," before running toward the fight, throwing the fireball at a tall Light Elf with long dark hair and a thin red scar down his face. He was standing over a Wizard, pushing his boot into the Wizard's neck and laughing. The fireball struck him in the neck, burning a hole that almost took off his head. He fell lifeless to the ground as Leira grew another fireball in her hand, magicals pouring forward in every direction.

Lois raised her wand over her head and yelled, "For Lacey Trader!" The agents behind her echoed her cry and they plunged across the open ground, back into the fight with their wands already casting spells, sending out long streams of gold wire dotted with razor sharp thorns.

The mercenaries fought back, unleashing their own weapons, crippling one side of the first wave of Oriceran magicals.

Boom!

The noise was loud enough to pop the ears of anyone standing nearby.

A portal opened and Queen Saria rushed forward, not waiting for the others, her eyes glowing and the buds on her crown a dark black. The old King of Oriceran was not far behind, running alongside his son. The queen raised her hands, bending her fingers in different directions, rippling the air as it wrapped around a Kilomea's neck, squeezing the life out of him.

The two trolls fought side by side, swinging their large, powerful paws at a trio of Light Elves. Nibbler managed to make contact with the midsection of one of them, ripping his chest open. Another rolled back his arm, letting a spray of fireballs loose, catching Nibbler's fur on fire. He screamed in pain as Yumfuck thundered in anger, stomping his feet and making short order of the Elve's head. It rolled across the ground like a forgotten bowling ball. He turned on the third Elf who retreated, running behind a Kilomea who tried to swing a sword at Yumfuck and came away with a stump. Yumfuck turned back to his friend who was lying on the ground, still smoldering. Nibbler looked at Yumfuck, pain in his eyes. "Fight on without me. Stop them from hurting anyone else."

"Nibbler, I'm not leaving you here. Shrink down. I'll get you help."

Nibbler moved his paw from his chest to show Yumfuck the gaping hole that was quickly bleeding out. "It's too late. I'm glad I got to know you and make you a friend. I'll see you again on the other side and we'll run through the tall grass and eat the petals off flowers." Nibbler's head fell back, and his eyes shut, his hand sliding off his chest.

Yumfuck stood up to his full height, bellowing out his pain and anger as Nibbler finally shrank back down to just five inches tall before turning into particles of light that drifted through the air like fireflies dancing on a breeze. Yumfuck watched his friend drift away and turned to move through the crowd of Wolfstan's army, slashing in his grief and tearing apart any magical foolish enough to not get out of the way.

Jackson pulled his knife out of a Kilomea, covered in slime and suddenly gasped, stumbling backward. His eyes widened and he opened his mouth, unable to take in air for a moment. Leira ran to her father's side, her back to him, fighting off a Witch who had seen him falter and was moving in with her wand raised. Leira let the energy surge through her, rattling the bracelet on her wrist. "Bury her," she whispered, setting an intention. A ribbon of energy rolled out, lifting the Witch high overhead and slammed her into the ground. Dirt fell onto her face as the Earth swallowed her whole, her arms outstretched, clawing at the sides till she was gone from view.

"You okay, Dad?" she called over her shoulder. She looked down at her wrist and saw the blisters from the bracelet. Jackson saw it too and grabbed her arm. "You're pushing it with the light. Be careful. Asking the light to take a life is very tricky business, even when it's justified. Choose carefully and fight without it as much as you can."

Jackson kissed his daughter's forehead, tasting the salty sweat. "Nibbler is dead. I can feel it."

"No... Yumfuck." She jerked her head around, trying to find the eight foot tall furry troll in the midst of the mayhem. But she couldn't see him.

"There's no time to worry right now. Go back into the fray and let's get this done." Jackson disappeared into the throng of magicals fighting each other as Leira turned to see who she could defend or stop from getting any further.

Wolfstan lowered his binoculars, worried. The battle was not going as he had planned. Too many of his mercenaries were falling on the field. Useless to his cause. The dark mist twisted up his legs, beckoning to him. A resigned look came over his entire countenance. "Fine. We'll do it your way. I will not lose today. Not again." The mist absorbed into his skin, feeding into his veins, creating a spidery black web that crept up his neck as his eyes turned a solid, shiny black.

The sky overhead turned neon green, casting everyone below in a glowing light that glinted off swords. A rip appeared in the sky, tearing open the veil between Terlingua, Texas and the world in between. Misshapen specters flew out from the crack in the sky, circling overhead. Dark mist swirled all around them as the fighting raged on down on the ground.

The old King of Oriceran saw what was happening and the color drained from his face. He raised his arms, his eyes glowing and called out. "Ancestors, brethren, grandfathers and grandmothers. Come to our rescue." He sent out a stream of energy as Queen Saria joined him with her magic, strengthening the plea. Leira shoved her foot into the chest of a Witch, pushing her to the ground and saw the pair, their magic coiling together toward the sky. She looked down at her wrist and the peeling blister. "This time join with their energy. Connect us to our past."

Her Jasper energy spiraled out of her, pulling her onto her toes as it swept up and around the old King and Queen Saria's magic. The Queen startled when she felt the power of Leira's magic, and she looked at Leira surprised. Her usually cool demeanor dropped, and she watched amazed as Leira's energy took her along for the ride, soaring into the heavens and sliding into the world in between and then beyond to the land of the dead. It spread out like water, calling out to the ancestors who had fallen in battle and asking them to rise again, for one last fight.

Faces appeared in the mist of Light Elves and Wizards who had lived long ago when the gates had been open. They answered without hesitation, their spectral images filling the sky, raising swords made of light to fight off the demons summoned by Wolfstan Humphrey.

The battle continued in the sky and along the flat Earth of Terlingua as the two sides fought to gain the advantage and win the day. Leira watched in amazement as the magicals from a distant past routed the pawns of the darkness in the world in between, driving them back into their eternal holding place.

But the fight was not faring as well on the ground for the allies. Too many were being driven back and dying. Leira saw Correk cornered by two Light Elves, a gash in his right arm. The Elves were too close for him to be able to raise his bow and she reacted fast. She slid the bracelet off her wrist and called on the light. *Help him. Help us. End this fight.*

A flash of light popped across the terrain, blinding everyone momentarily, shrinking back down and spinning around Leira.

The two Elves in front of Correk were momentarily distracted and he took advantage and pulled out the knife he always kept in his boot. With one slash at just the right height, their fight was over, and they toppled like heavy trees face first into the dirt. He looked to find the source of the light and saw Leira standing in the middle of it, transfixed and screamed. "Leira, no!" But it was too late. Her light was spinning upward, joining with the dead still swirling overhead.

Help us. End the fight.

The ghostly lights gathered around her, enveloping the Jasper Elf as Correk fought his way toward her. The ghosts descended, growing larger till they covered the battlefield. Each of the magicals who had agreed to fight for money and betray their own kind froze where they were, the light seeping into their skin and back out of their eyes and their nose and their mouth. They trembled where they stood, dropping their weapons as their heads rocked back and the light poured out of them, following the ancestors back toward the land of the dead. Leira's magic was still intertwined with theirs, following them toward the opening in the sky as the light continued to swirl around her figure on the ground.

Correk stepped over the bodies of the fallen mercenaries, reaching out for Leira, tears staining his cheeks. But Louie made it to her first. He was listening to the urgent shouts from the sword that filled his head. *Take her hand, pull her down. Hold the sword in your other hand. Ground her.*

He grasped her hand and felt a jolt of electricity pass through him and a searing pain run down his spine and out every limb, but he didn't let go. The energy continued to pulse through him, rattling his teeth as it ran toward the sword in his other hand, siphoning it off.

The ancestors looked back at Leira's light following them and down at the ground and hesitated. The specter of an ancient Jasper Elf emerged at the front and blew into the air, his cheeks puffing out. The wind pushed Leira's light back even as she felt something familiar wrapping around her, urging her to return. *Family.*

The ghosts slowly blended back into light, seeping through the rip in the sky as it disappeared. The light around Leira slowed down, dimming till it was absorbed into the scar on her belly. Louie finally let go of her hand and fell backward, knocking his head, still hanging onto his sword. He was sucking in air with his eyes squeezed shut, waiting for the pain to subside. Jackson found him and put Louie's head in his lap. "Thank you for saving my child," he said, as Louie gritted his teeth. Jackson let his magic wind around Louie's body, easing the pain till he could open his eyes. "Welcome back," said Jackson, smiling at him.

Correk finally made it to Leira just as she was about to drop to the ground. He put out his arms and caught her, lifting her up amid the battlefield, clogged with bodies and magicals still barely standing. "I almost lost you," he whispered into her hair.

Leira opened her eyes. "Better me than you," she said faintly. "I can't walk this life without you. It would be too long." She laid her head against his chest, her heart pounding. "Let's get back to our porch," she said, licking her dry lips. "You can put me down. I can still walk off the field."

"Kate!" Lois weaved her way around the fallen soldiers to the crumpled body of the fallen Atlantean. She knelt down next to Kate's body, touching the skin. "She's still warm. Maybe there's a chance."

"No, Lois. She's gone. Let her be at peace." Patsy put her hand on Lois' wand and pointed to the crisscross of wounds on Kate's chest. "She was a spirited girl and a good fighter, even if she asked a lot of questions." Patsy tried to smile, blinking back tears.

"Oh damn, Patsy, now you've got me going." Lois took off her glasses and wiped her face. She patted the top of her hair and growled. "Well, dammit it all. Someone blew a hole straight through the top of my bouffant."

"You didn't smell your hair burning?"

"Look around. There was too much burning hair to know whose was whose." She stood up and waved to a cluster of Silver Griffin agents nearby. "Make sure she gets carried off the field pronto. She was a good friend to the Silver Griffins. Don't leave her body unattended."

"Where is Wolfstan Humphrey?" yelled Queen Saria.

Leira stood up and felt a little lightheaded, hanging onto Correk as she looked up toward the structure where he had been seen last. A crowd made their way up there, slowed down by the debris of bodies in their way. They approached with caution; their weapons drawn just in case.

But when they arrived all they found was a pile of clothes and ashes. "Do you think he's dead?" asked Lucius.

"I hope so," said Ariana, pocketing her wand. "But if he's not, I'll find him and light him up myself." A breeze picked up, scattering the ashes. "Enjoy hell, Wolfstan," said Ariana. "You earned it."

"Your arm," said Leira, taking a better look at the gash still oozing on Correk's bicep.

"You two go home. Take Yumfuck with you," said the King of Oriceran. "There are enough magicals here to take away our dead and help the others. You've earned the right to sit down. You saved us all. Thank you," said the king, kneeling before them. Queen Saria joined her husband and knelt down, bowing her head and then looking up at Leira. "You are the finest warrior I have ever known. It's a privilege to know you," she said as the buds on her crown turned snow white. She stood and waved her arms, opening a portal to the small kitchen on N Street in Washington. "Go home," she said.

Leira looked around for Yumfuck, who had shrunk down to five inches to make his way more easily to her.

She scooped him up and held him close to her cheek. "I'm so sorry. Your friend."

Yumfuck let out a baleful cry as she pressed him against her throat and held him there. Jackson gently hugged his daughter. "I'll stop by soon. Take a few days off and find something fun to do that doesn't involve magic. Advice from your old man."

Leira took Correk's hand and stepped through to her kitchen, the floor squeaking, making her smile. "Home at last," she said, as Correk followed her and the portal closed, leaving them in the silence. "Let's go to bed and just lie there. I'm keeping Yumfuck with us tonight."

"After you," said Correk, as she headed for the stairs, glancing at the pictures of their family as she passed them.

CHAPTER TWENTY-NINE

"I'll be fine, you'll see." Winland Turner hugged her father, who was doing his best to look unconcerned. She watched with amusement as he tap, tap, tapped his cane on the old run in his library. "It's time we all moved on."

Turner Underwood cleared his throat and looked out the tall window, his eyebrows waggling. "What about this Erickson? He was never caught, you know. He's still a threat out there."

"Duly noted. First, I was trained by you so there's that. Second, you taught me to never put off life. To live it to the fullest because you never know what's going to happen. I plan to take that advice. Third, we may never find Erickson. He could be dead. He could have moved on after he saw what he did. Or he could come for us, and if that happens, we'll deal with it on that day."

Turner let out a sign. "Sounds like something I would have said. It's to be East Calico Rock in Arkansas? Not a bad choice. A ghost town that's set off by itself in the Ozarks, not too far from a real town."

"Dad, did you check out the town when I wasn't looking?"

"I felt a certain responsibility to make sure you checked off all the boxes. I was pleasantly surprised to see that you had. Did you know that the fishing in White River is supposed to be superb? Maybe I'll get a cabin nearby."

Winland tilted her head to one side and smiled. "You do you, Dad. What will you do with your turn of the century New York City once it's emptied out?"

"Ah, that's an easy one. There will always be magicals in need of refuge of some sort. And when they do, I will be there, or Correk after I'm gone. No frowns, my dear. It's still a long way off but someday I'll be in that lovely vault near my old friend Lacey." He walked his oldest daughter out of the library and down the hall toward the door to an entirely other house. "Or," he said, throwing up his hands, "maybe I'll keep it for grand parties. They could go on for days and everyone could have their own brownstone. You could come back and visit and help me host."

"I have plans to run for office in the new town, but I'm sure I could fit it into my schedule."

"Public service," said Turner, standing straighter, a look of pride on his face. "Well, you get that sense of duty from my side of the family."

Winland took her father's arm and walked with him, leaning in to smell the familiar scent of patchouli and whiskey. "It's a new day. A fresh start for a lot of us. I'm actually very excited to see what comes next."

"Me too, daughter. Many more adventures await us."

CHAPTER THIRTY

"We're never going to get any sleep tonight. There has to be fifty trolls crammed into that room." Correk leaned over the side of the bed looking at the floor.

"They're bite size. Fifty fit in there easily."

There was a general cheer that rose from the room just underneath them followed by, "Yumfuck! Yumfuck! Yumfuck!" and a hearty, "Aloha motherfuckers!"

"Yeah, you're right," said Leira, pulling Correk back toward her. "Let's make good use of the night, then."

Correk smiled and arched a brow. "Why, Leira Berens you are always thinking," he said, pulling her into his arms.

Leira kissed him and pulled back to look into his deep blue eyes. "What a good life. Makes me wonder what the future holds…"

"Let's ponder that tomorrow."

There was a loud bang as something heavy hit the floor and a chorus of shushing. Leira gave a crooked smile. "Let's ponder that tomorrow too. The future can wait just a little while longer."

Ossonia pressed her face up against the veil, straining to see through it. She had been searching for another thin place since the old one on New York Avenue had been destroyed. Days were spent sliding down different holes in the ooze inside the world in between, searching. *Nothing.*

She opened her mouth to scream, but there was no sound. She squeezed her eyes shut and thought of Perrom. She opened her eyes and watched a new passageway open up. The young Light Elf stepped through and gasped, rushing to the edge of the veil. There on the other side was the Dark Forest.

Perrom! Perrom! She beat her fists against the invisible barrier, stopping suddenly when he looked around as if he had heard something. But he went back to chopping wood, lost to her again. *Not forever. Somehow, not forever.*

Ariana looked out over the tents that had been set up to house the Witches and Wizards who were still in need of refuge. New identities for the misplaced Silver Griffin agents was going to take some time. Uncle Felix was tagging along with her, riding up front in the golf cart as they took a tour. "You know, I think it's time we expanded our family," she said, waving to a tall Witch with long dark hair. "New blood in an old system will help both sides."

Uncle Felix let out a short laugh. "And if we ever need to go back to warring with Leira Berens again, it can't hurt to have some old agents on our side."

"Just in case," said Ariana. "A good Plan B."

The story is far from over. It's quite a few years later and Leira and Correk returning to Austin to solve a murder and help some friends out. The adventure continues in <u>Return of Magic</u>

Get sneak peeks, exclusive giveaways, behind the scenes content, and more. PLUS you'll be notified of special **one day only fan pricing** on new releases.

Sign up today to get free stories.

Visit: https://marthacarr.com/read-free-stories/

I hope you enjoyed the conclusion to Wolfstan's story and the dilemma of mixing magic with technology and then stirring in the need for power to prove self-worth. Leira finds a bigger meaning of family and just how important being there for those right around you can be. Same goes for old Lucius. Wolfstan may have missed the point. I threw in everything I had for that final battle and felt my heart racing or breaking as I wrote the words.

Everyone grew in one direction or another, good and bad, in the completion to this part of the story.

So, what comes next? That's a good question.

Originally, my plan was to go to Italy for part of last summer and work on those middle years when Izzie is born. (If this is coming as news to you and you're asking, who's Izzie, check out the series, The School of Necessary Magic). But then, the world changed, and a pandemic struck, and borders closed…

For now, in book 13, *Return of Magic*, we will jump ahead in time to the Brownstone era and rejoin Leira and

Correk when they suddenly have to return to Austin, Texas, – their roots – to solve a deadly mystery and help out some old friends. Look for the return of some familiar faces and a few new ones.

And then there's Izzie… (I can't say anything else. No spoilers, of course)

Stay tuned and keep reading to see what happens next as new adventures begin and a few remaining questions get answered.

Maybe next summer I will get my Italian trip, or I will be sitting in my new Secret Garden that will be getting installed in the spring. Based on the events of 2020, I have given up making long range plans, at least for now. I know that I'll find happiness and gratitude, and work through the rest with others, no matter what comes.

That's a good place to be anyway. Totally in the present, paying attention to the people right around me and writing fun stories full of humor and adventure. Plus, there's that garden.

I stand in the backyard a lot these days and picture where everything will go and feel my own personal roots growing deeper in one spot. My old idea was to rent and to always be able to move quickly. Part of it was my love of new people, new places. Part of it was being a journalist in search of a new story. And part of it was growing up poor and in an interesting household and never really learning how to have roots.

All that has changed.

I've figured out that it's okay to keep moving around if you want – that's got a lot of perks and boy, do I have stories to tell. And it's also okay to stay in one place that kind of suits me like Austin does, and figure out that parts of it I will love and parts of it I will not at all and the rest will be somewhere in the middle. The deal is to figure out how much sits in the 'love' part and if that is bigger – maybe you're already home. More adventures to follow.

Thank you for not only reading this story but also to the back where we have our *Author Notes*!

I know a little about Martha's backstory, so I know a little about the moving around she did. While I moved, it was rarely an action to go discover but more a reaction of needing a different place.

Whether it is a growing family or the need to get away from family.

Until Vegas.

Our twins (Jacob and Joseph) were heading out. One was going to Arlington, the other to Texarkana. Judith and I were heading back west, but not to California (she kinda wanted to go there, but I wasn't happy with their tax system whatsoever).

Nope, we found a place in the city of lights and parties. Las Vegas, Nevada.

And not just any place in the city. Nope, somehow my introverted little butt ended up living in the MIDDLE of the damned Strip where $80 steaks and $12 Starbucks (!!!) were just downstairs.

You know, I got that Keurig working really quick to solve the $12 Starbuck problem.

As for the $80 steaks, that was Maestro's, and I am overweight because…let's just say it was too convenient and too close. I could have used a few more steps between that restaurant and my front door.

(It actually cost less than $80.00 for the steak, but then add the baked potato, a Coke, and a cake slice plus tip. Well, I didn't go too often, but I remember one time I just HAD to have a steak, and it was there, amIright?)

For the next couple of years, it was like living inside a party every damned day. Including (during the summertime on weekends) the outdoor THUMP THUMP THUMP of the bass from the pool parties at the nearby Cosmopolitan and Park etc., etc.

Drove me sorta nuts. Judith loved it.

Then COVID and my slow spiral into a deep funk. Now the everlasting party that never stopped gave way to the everlasting nothing that required me to get in a car to actually see any other human beings. The Strip was shut down. No stores, no restaurants, nothing.

Not even CVS or Walgreens was close and open anymore.

By the time Las Vegas sort of started opening the Strip, I had implemented a plan and ~~suckered~~, encouraged, my wife to enjoy a house out in Henderson. All the fun of Vegas is just twenty-five minutes away, and none of the pain of living with no backyard, balcony, or burgers!

I'm glad to be here in Henderson since our governor is

pushing people to stay home again for the second wave of COVID. I feel like I can be optimistic because nature doesn't care. The birds will come drink from our little water fountains no matter what the governor suggests we do, and now I just need to work on my wife to want a man kitchen outside.

You know, that massive, all-brick cool stuff where you can cook, it has a small fridge, and you feel one with nature as the steak sizzles on the grill?

Sure, let's ignore that I won't cook in the heat…or the cold…or the wind. I won't cook when tired, when busy with work, when I don't feel like going to the grocery, thawing out meat, or cleaning.

Huh.

I guess I'm not getting a man-kitchen. *Dammit.*

Have a fantastic holiday season while I go and think about how I can accomplish my next big thing in the back-yard now that I have one. Too filled up to have a basketball court or an outdoor office for a man-cave…

I think maybe the enjoyment of thinking is going to have to be the end goal on this one.

Ad Aeternitatem,

Michael

If smart phones and GPS rule the world - why am I hunting a magic compass to save the planet?

Austin Detective Maggie Parker has seen some weird things in her day, but finding a surly gnome rooting through her garage beats all.

Her world is about to be turned upside down in a frantic search for 4 Elementals.

Each one has an artifact that can keep the Earth humming along, but they need her to unite them first.

Unless the forces against her get there first.

<u>AVAILABLE ON AMAZON AND IN KINDLE UNLIMITED!</u>

www.ingramcontent.com/pod-product-compliance
Lightning Source LLC
Chambersburg PA
CBHW050250110726
47898CB00007B/2349